LORD TEDRIC RETURNS

This time Tedric leads a rebellion to wrest the power of the crown from the diabolical Carey family, aided by his trusty allies—a blue-furred Wykzl, a subman, a deposed lord, a near-human robot, and a kidnapped princess. And it is only the beginning. For as the battle rages, an even greater, more malevolent force is threatening the galaxy—a threat that Tedric can only begin to comprehend. Here is space fantasy at its best, filled with amazing machinery and even more amazing aliens, in an action-packed adventure with all the excitement that made the "Doc" Smith odysseys so pupular.

SPACE PIRATES

LORD TEDRIC #2

SPACE PIRATES

GORDON EKLUND

SF

ace books

A Division of Charter Communications Inc.
A GROSSET & DUNLAP COMPANY
360 Park Avenue South
New York, New York 10010

An ACE Book
by arrangement with
Baronet Publishing Company

First Ace printing: March 1980

2 4 6 8 0 9 7 5 3 1
Manufactured in the United States of America

CONTENTS

1. Lady Alyc Carey   7
2. Lord Tedric   31
3. Space Pirates of Quicksilver   55
4. Stone Castle   83
5. The Black Beast   97
6. Narabia   113
7. The Destruction of Vishnu   137
8. Mo-leete Makes an Offer   151
9. Emperor Matthew I   163
10. Against the Fleet   181
11. Beating the Odds   211

1 LADY ALYC CAREY

Even before the space pirates of Quicksilver made her their prisoner, Lady Alyc Carey, only daughter of the richest family in the Empire of Man, loathed the pulse and pattern of her nineteen common-years of changeless existence. She yearned for something different, whether glorious or terrible, ugly or lovely, sweet or foul, any one thing that might interrupt the apparently eternal click-clack rhythm of what she was forced to call life.

This was her desire, but what made it truly dreadful for Alyc was her nearly certain knowledge that the odds stood at more than two hundred fifty billion to one that no such interruption would occur.

That figure (two hundred fifty billion) was the present estimated human female population of the Empire. In other words, as Alyc well knew, no remarkable changes had been known to occur in any woman's life.

Why should Lady Alyc herself be any more fortunate?

That she eventually was, that the space pirates captured her, in no way altered the inexorability of those odds. Capture by space pirates was a freakish deviation in the law of probabilities. As pleased as she was that it had happened—especially, that it had happened to her—Lady Alyc never once lost sight of her own good luck.

To fully comprehend the limited nature of Lady Alyc's life before her capture, it would first be necessary to understand two related items, one general and one particular.

The first of these, the general, was the place of human females as a gender within the Empire of Man during the last years of the reign of Emperor Kane IV. The second of these was the particular position of Lady Alyc Carey, granddaughter of Fraken Carey, daughter of Melor Carey, younger sister of Matthew Carey. Alyc's family was the most powerful in the Empire.

Women were not permitted to wield power in the Empire.

This second point was one that even historians tended to ignore. Women had been regarded as a secondary, a passive gender for so many centuries that few people recalled that this had not always been the case.

For instance, in the area of space exploration alone, of the forty-nine crew members aboard the starship *Viola* undertaking the first N-space voyage at velocities in excess of light, twenty-nine had been women. ·

Detailed records indicated—extremely detailed records, it was true—that the eighth ruling potentate of the Empire of Man was actually one Empress Neva I. She reigned fewer than two common-years and was assassinated by her own second son.

It was the same son, Emperor Kane I, who issued a declaration of war against the neighboring space nation of the blue-furred Wykzl. This war, which was to last slightly more than one thousand years, ended in a Wykzl victory.

If historians ever bothered to study the subject, they might well have discovered a connection right there: war meant the subjugation of women, and eternal war—or so it usually seemed—meant eternal subjugation.

There were few areas, objectively, where men and women were not equal. War—killing and being killed—happened to be one of these.

With war, too, came the need for bodies. Submen could be soldiers, but someone had to lead them.

That meant men.

And to produce men—easily, quickly, effortlessly —women were needed. Live women, preferably young, not dead ones, whatever age.

Within fifty common-years of Kane's declaration of war, women had been reduced to the role of suppliers. They bore children, who either entered the military, if they were men, or produced additional children, if they were women.

To ensure the easy fulfillment of their feminine procreative role, women were made subject to a firm, detailed code of conduct. Among other things, the code stated that:

No unmarried woman shall speak to any unmarried man without the permission of her father. (The reason for this, quite simply, was to preserve the strongest possible breeding lines. In war, strength meant life.)

No woman, married or unmarried, shall hold property, possess credit, or provide necessary services. (The reason, in this instance: money, jobs, and property took time away from childbearing.)

No woman shall glide, swim, skate, fly, run, hike, or engage in any fashion in an active sport or game. (People who did such things sometimes got hurt; an injured woman was a useless woman.)

And so on.

Besides, there were always the submen.

The rigid code of conduct applied only to human females. By the time of Emperor Kane IV, at least fifty percent of the imperial population was composed of submen and subwomen, descendants of successful genetic experiments designed to increase the native intelligence of various of Earth's original animal species: monkeys, great apes, dogs, domestic and untamed cats. Throughout the Empire of Man, submen performed those common and menial tasks that could not be accomplished by robots or machines. Fully human beings of both sexes were thus set free to live lives of meaningful idleness and contemplation. During the Wykzl War, practically, this meant that the men served as officers in the military, but the war was now over, and the idleness of most men had become a good deal less meaningful than before.

Still, the existence of this separate, less than fully human race made it possible to devise and carry out the terms of a rigid code of feminine conduct.

When a fully human unmarried male wished to speak to an unmarried woman, he went and found a subwoman. When a fully human male wished to have a woman to help with his business, he hired a subwoman.

When a fully human wished to engage in co-educational sports, he got a subwoman to serve as his partner.

It worked well. No one objected to this arrangement. It was part of the imperial way of life at the time of Kane IV.

The only trouble was, now that the war had ended, this code no longer made any sense at all. Its *raison d'etre* had expired. Bodies were not needed to fight the war; the population of the Empire boomed beyond control.

Few people recognized these facts. One of them was Lady Alyc Carey.

But what could she do? Alyc was merely a woman.

She was also blind.

The accident had occurred some seven and a half years subsequent to her birth. So she remembered the visible world; it continued to live in her memories if not in her eyes. But it was a world frozen in time. It never grew or changed. Her father was still one hundred-twenty years old. Her brother was a little boy, despite a surprisingly deep voice and amazingly big hands. Trees stayed green. Flowers didn't die.

The accident had occurred because Melor Carey had dared to violate the established code of feminine conduct. He let his unmarried daughter leave the precincts of her own home. She was only seven and he was very rich and powerful. He saw no good reason why he—and she—shouldn't do whatever they wanted.

The trip had taken them through space to the star KC97L, which, as all astronomers predicted, was about to go nova.

It was expected to be the most stunning cosmic sight of its age. A dozen starships occupied by astronomers, physicists, and astrogators had flocked to the spot. Melor Carey was one of the few non-scientists permitted in the vicinity. (One other, the Crown Prince, Randow, had come all the way from Earth as the official representative of his father's court.) Matthew and Alyc Carey were certainly the only children.

The imperial navy was also present in force, because the imperial navy was always present everywhere in force.

KC97L decided to go nova some fourteen minutes before the predicted time and caught nearly everyone by surprise.

And someone aboard the *Blue Eagle*, the Carey family shuttle, accidentally left a porthole unsealed.

That last seemed impossible. Melor Carey simply did not allow mistakes to be committed anywhere near his presence. Nine robot technicians had later been disconnected as a result. Two submen servants were discorporated.

Actually, it was the fault of none of these creatures. Alyc Carey had opened the porthole herself. Before she could confess, the disconnections and discorporations had been carried out. Normally, that would have been murder, but Melor Carey was permitted to make mistakes where he allowed none himself.

Alyc was curious. When the nova went off, she wanted to see it. Not on a screen. Not two-dimensionally. Not shrunken or edited or less than real.

She wanted to see it—the event.

So she opened the porthole.

The nova exploded. (Too early, it was true; perhaps Alyc never really intended to go through with the whole thing.)

She alone saw *it* occur.

And she went blind.

But only afterward. For one infinitesimally brief microsecond, Alyc witnessed the raw naked power of the cosmos. It was a sight that frightened her and which she never forgot.

After the accident, Alyc went to Earth for treatment. The medical technicians of the imperial court risked disconnection by pronouncing her permanently blind. Melor Carey took her home to the family planet, Milrod Eleven in the Quixmass sector. At one time, Milrod Eleven had housed a population of three million, but after Fraken Carey grew rich and powerful, he had ordered all his neighbors to move. The Careys now occupied the entire world, its ghostly cities and abandoned farms, but they seldom strayed far beyond the traditional boundaries of their own homestead.

It was anticipated by those who knew her story and the fact of the rigid feminine code of conduct that Alyc Carey (now officially a *Lady* by order of Emperor Kane) would live out the remaining hundred or so years of her life as a lonely invalid. From the age of eight until she was nineteen, that was pretty much the case.

Her brother Matthew, three years older than she, spent his vacations from the imperial schools on Earth at the family homestead. Alyc didn't like Matthew and spoke to him only often enough to make him irritated.

Other children came from Earth and elsewhere to play with her and serve her company. Alyc alternately ignored them or heaped abuse on them and their families. She never played with any of them. Once, when she was fourteen, she stabbed a persistent playmate in the chest, nearly killing the boy. Nobody knew where she'd gotten the knife (actually, she'd made it herself), and after that, her visitors were fewer.

Her father was home only when business and politics failed to take him somewhere else. She enjoyed playing chess and other games with him, but when they talked, she couldn't bear the pain and guilt that always filled his voice.

Her two good friends were Kuevee, a robot, and Kisha, a subwoman. Kuevee tended the family flower garden, where vegetation from half-a-hundred alien worlds grew in chaotic splendor. Kuevee always made her laugh and she respected his incredible knowledge of alien botany.

Her relationship with Kisha, her personal servant, was closer. She talked constantly with Kisha and rarely had to listen. Kisha had been given to Alyc shortly after the accident, so she was not part of the frozen world, either. Kisha's great - great - great - great - great - great - great - great - great - great grandparents were lions. When she wanted, when she was alone with Alyc in the garden, Kisha could make a roaring noise that shook the highest trees.

Alyc spent most of her time alone. She enjoyed being with Kuevee or Kisha, but more than anything, she liked sitting beside the rattling brook that ran behind the big house and listening to the voices that spoke in her mind.

They may have been her best friends of all.

She had first heard the voices on the *Blue Eagle* immediately following the accident. They had never gone away. What they said, who they were, how they spoke to her, Alyc never revealed. She heard voices but knew enough never to tell anyone, not even Kuevee or Kisha, of their existence.

She often dreamed of how her life would some-day change and be absolutely different from what it had always been before. Even though she dreamed, she was well aware of the odds of two hundred fifty billion to one that this would never happen. On her nineteenth birthday, she went to see her father and asked again about the space voyage. She had asked the first time when she was sixteen and again when she was seventeen and eighteen. Every year on her birthday, Melor Carey said, "Whatever you want for a birthday present, just tell me and I promise you'll have it," and she told him she wanted to take a voyage through space.

But that was in strict violation of the code of feminine conduct.

So Melor told her no, as much as it hurt him to do it.

This year, on her nineteenth birthday, she found him in his usual place in the big house in the electric room. She called it that because all she could recall from her frozen childhood world of memories of her father's office was the maze of wires and circuitry. She pictured her father as she recalled him: a short, wiry, bushy white-haired man, with slim hands, thick brows, and an expression of incredible intensity.

He spoke from his desk imprisoned in a cage of

black wires. "I'll be with you as soon as I finish this call, Alyc."

She nodded, found the easy chair in its usual place, and sat down. While Melor Carey talked with Earth, Alyc listened passively to the voices in her own mind.

She heard him click the receiver and turned her attention toward him.

He sighed. "Matthew may be coming home soon."

"I thought he was supposed to stay on Earth and take care of those criminals."

"He was. They got away from him. Can you believe that, Alyc? All three men—and a Wykzl—escaped from the imperial prison on Earth."

"I don't suppose it was Matthew's fault in the least," she said sarcastically. Despite her disinterest in any affairs beyond the precincts of her own home, Alyc disliked Matthew intensely enough to enjoy hearing her father berate him.

"So he's ready to claim at great length," said Melor.

"And you believe him?"

He heaved a sigh. "Of course not. The damn fool. Somebody had better hope that I live at least as long as my father, because if I die and Matthew takes over the family interests, the Empire is going to be in awfully sad shape."

"I'm sure you'll live forever, as long as it suits you."

He laughed.

So then she told him openly that today was her birthday and what she wanted as a gift was to take a voyage through space.

Melor, of course, had heard this plea three times before and was immediately ready to object. She heard him move away from his tangled cage and approach her chair. She felt his hairy hand (as she remembered it) on her bare shoulder. "Alyc, I wish it could be so."

"Then why can't it?" She turned her face toward him, knowing how deeply it stung him to see her dead eyes.

"Because of many things. Because of what happened the last time, for one thing."

"But I can't go blind again. I am already blind. I'm safe."

"No." He moved away from her now, pacing the length of the room. "I can't expect you to understand, but it was very, very wrong of me ever to let you leave home, even when you were just a child. For me to do it now, when you're grown up, would be worse than wrong."

"But who can say that? You're the most powerful man in the Empire. When you sneeze, the Emperor jumps. I've heard you say that often enough."

"This has nothing to do with power or with the Emperor. I would know that I was wrong. That should be enough."

"And if I promise not to look at any more novas?"

She heard the intake of his breath and knew that she had hurt him again. He said, "That's not the point either, Alyc. What's wrong is wrong no matter how many precautions we take. No one aboard would speak with you, an unmarried woman on a voyage by herself."

"I don't want to speak with anyone."

He continued to pace. "Besides, I just can't see any good reason. I've traveled as much as any non-navy man alive, and I can tell you. Space is a barren place. Any one planet, even if it's inhabited, is pretty much the same as the one next to it. If you go on a voyage, you won't see anything you haven't already seen here on Milrod."

"Father, I won't be *seeing* anything. Have you forgotten? I'm as blind as a bat."

Again, the sharp intake of breath. She knew she was being cruel but felt he had forced her into it. Especially with Matthew home, the sameness was unbearable. She had to get away or go mad and in the Empire of Man, space was the only place to go.

"No," he said finally. He had drawn close and touched her again. "I just can't permit it, Alyc. For your sake, not mine. For your reputation."

In the end, it took Alyc six common-months to force Melor Carey to give in. The times before, when she was sixteen and seventeen and eighteen, she had accepted his refusal at face value, but her desperation had grown. She pounded away at her father every chance she got. Fortunately, with Matthew now home, Melor was often home, too. She spent more time in his office than in the five years previous. Eventually, as she knew she must, she won the battle.

Passage was booked for her aboard the liner, *Oceania,* and a special stop was arranged to pick her up at Milrod Eleven. The *Oceania* was the largest and most luxurious ship in the imperial service. (Melor Carey owned full title to it.) Alyc, it was decided, would remain aboard the liner for one full round trip, a duration of some nine common-months. In that time the *Oceania* would stop and visit eighteen occupied worlds. Melor Carey tried to convince his daughter to travel with a companion. He suggested several unmarried daughters of friendly noble families, but Alyc said she didn't want to ruin the reputation of an innocent girl. Melor then urged her to travel in the company of a husband and wife. He mentioned a number of names, but again Alyc demurred. For every name Melor raised, Alyc raised a firm objection. The people were too crude, rude, stupid, foul-smelling, or debauched.

In the end, Melor Carey gave up. Alyc would travel accompanied only by her personal servant, Kisha. She asked if Kuevee, the robot, could go too, but Melor explained that imperial regulations forbade the transport of robots on civilian ships. Besides, Kuevee's services were needed in the alien garden. Alyc said that she understood.

Her brother, Matthew, left Milrod Eleven aboard a private ship two days before Alyc's own scheduled departure. He returned to the Earth to assume com-

mand of a squadron in the Imperial Corps of the One
Hundred.

Alyc took advantage of her two final days alone
to say good-bye to Kuevee and the flowers, plants,
trees, and ferns that formed so integral a part of her
former life.

Then the day came when the shuttle lifted off
Milrod Eleven to carry her to the *Oceania* in orbit in
space above. Her father accompanied her. Alyc chattered constantly to keep his spirits up. She knew how
terrified he must feel, like a man who had created a
monster he could no longer control. (Kisha had once
read her an old book about such a man.) Alyc sympa-
thized, but she was overjoyed herself. This was a
change. An alteration in the pulse and pattern of her
life. A rend in the fabric of her tedious existence.

She had succeeded at last in breaking those terrible odds.

Or so she thought. At first. By the time the
Oceania swung into orbit around its ninth inhabited
world, she knew how wrong she was.

It was Melor who was right. They were all the
same. There was nothing different here. She was
bored, sick, bored, tired, bored. She wanted to go
home.

Most days, she spent in her room. There, if nothing else, she could talk to Kisha or else listen to the
voices in her head. They were oddly different here,
not always the same voices she had heard at home,
but no less comforting or disturbing because of that.

Still, there were times when she felt that she should go out. She ate dinner in the ship's dining room on five occasions and twice visited planets when the *Oceania* stopped.

At these times, she learned exactly how changeless everything was and also how wrong Melor Carey could be.

No one ignored her or snubbed her or acted disgusted by her conduct. That she could have endured —that, truthfully, was what she preferred. Instead, it was their endless attention that she loathed. Melor Carey had erred. He had simultaneously underestimated the lure of his own name and power and overestimated the strength of an anachronistic code of behavior.

Alyc, of course, despised everyone she met on board the *Oceania*. People were smug, dull, complacent, tedious, and they talked and talked, without point or purpose. Once, at dinner, she yawned in a famous noblewoman's face. Another time, while visiting the planet Spartacus, she spit on a young duke's shoes. Nobody dared correct her behavior, but nobody left her alone either. They knew who she was. One complimentary word from Lady Alyc Carey was worth a crown of gold to them. Alyc never said a nice word to anyone, but they wouldn't give up.

Between the tenth and eleventh planets on their itinerary, in the gray realm of N-space, which Alyc vividly recalled from her previous trip, the space pirates of Quicksilver struck.

Alyc had heard of them before. She didn't usually pay much attention to the transitory phenomena that filled most newstapes, but during Matthew's recent visit, he had spoken of little else. The space pirates, it was said, raided backworld planets, burning and looting, and attacked defenseless naval vessels, burning and killing. The pirates were terrible men, renegades for certain, with their actual identities and origins well-concealed behind masks. The space pirates of Quicksilver were costing the Carey family interests great chunks of money. Matthew insisted they must be wiped out at any cost.

He had gone to Earth to head a squadron designed to do just that.

Unfortunately, between the tenth and eleventh planets on the tour, Alyc met the pirates long before her brother ever found them.

No warning was given. No shots were fired. No heatgun blasts. No alarm was sounded.

Alyc sat on a couch in her stateroom and listened to the voices in her head, while Kisha prepared a gown to be worn that night to dinner. (Alyc had decided, stubbornly, to risk the dining room one more time.) The stateroom viewscreen came to life. Alyc heard only a tinny voice. "This is Captain Clausen speaking. I have been ordered to inform you that our ship, the *Oceania,* has today been illegally boarded by a band of outlaws calling themselves the pirates of Quicksilver. It was my decision to offer no armed resistence to these men, and they have promised in turn to harm none of you. However, all passengers are requested to report at once to the ship's central lounge. You must bring all the valuables in your possession, including credit and jewelry, when you come. I'm afraid the pirates have appropriated both a passenger list and a description of all belongings. Unless all of you report as ordered, the ship will be detained until you do."

"We will not go," said Kisha's firm voice.

"Of course we will," said Alyc.

"But these pirates are terrible, terrible men."

"How do we know? We haven't met them."

"When he was home, Matthew spoke of nothing else. He is determined to fight them at any cost."

"What Matthew knows about anything, you could fit into a peashell."

"Your father will have me discorporated if I allow you to face danger."

But Alyc was already on her feet. She moved toward the stateroom door. "You'll have to stop me, Kisha." She knew, being blind, she could never locate the ship's central lounge without help.

Kisha knew this, too. After first heaving an exasperated sigh, she said, "Wait until I have gathered our valuables."

"They do have a list of names, you know," said Alyc.

"Why do you think I am allowing you to do this?" Actually, despite her years of service, Kisha had not yet discovered a way of saying no to Alyc Carey. Neither had anyone else.

The two women left their stateroom hand-in-hand and proceeded into the corridor.

There was panic here. Alyc sensed it, like an odor, as soon as they moved. People wandered aimlessly. No one seemed to know whether to run and hide or march and obey. Alyc's presence seemed to soothe them. Kisha carried their valuables in an open pouch. Alyc acted as an example. Seeing her compliance, people rushed to do likewise.

Because of this, although Alyc and Kisha were among the very first to reach the lounge, a thick crowd soon formed around them. It was hot in the room. The hum of nervous voices hurt Alyc's ears. She tried to pay more attention to the gentler voices that spoke privately in her mind.

Then someone began to read from a list of names. People were told, when they heard their name read, they were to come forward and have their valuables checked. The man reading the names was clearly a pirate, and he had at least one other person helping him. Alyc had a strange sensation that she'd heard the first voice before in her life. If a passenger, when called, failed to produce sufficient valuables to satisfy the pirates, he was sent away again.

The list was alphabetical. It wasn't too long, therefore, when the pirate said, "Lady Alyc Carey." There was immediate silence in the room, as if everyone present had taken a deep breath all at once. The pirate's voice registered stunned surprise. He had not anticipated uttering such a famous name.

The crowd of passengers swirled around so

tightly that Alyc was sure the pirates could not see her. She tugged on Kisha's arm. "Lead me forward, please."

"No, Alyc, I can go alone."

"It was my name they called."

"But—"

"Lead me."

The crowd parted to let her pass. Alyc heard the scraping of shoes. She touched no one as she moved but could feel them close, hear their controlled breathing. They feared her, but they also stood in awe.

There was an open space at the front of the room. Captain Clausen was there—she recognized the familiar wheezing of his breath—and two men she did not immediately know. There was a fourth person, who sounded like Kuevee. A robot? A robot pirate?

Kisha pressed down on her palm. Alyc glided to a stop.

"Is this woman the daughter of Melor Carey?" asked the individual Alyc thought might be a robot.

"Yes, and Matthew's sister." This was the voice that had spoken her name. Once again, she thought it was strangely familiar. She knew this person—this pirate. But from where? Or when?

"She's blind," the robot said.

"It's the result of a childhood accident."

That provided the clue. Childhood. Why, yes, of course, thought Alyc, now I know who you are. The voice belonged to her childhood. It was one of the boys her father had brought to play with her. She remembered, because she had liked him more than the others, but Matthew had fought with him and, after a few visits, the boy had not come again.

The shock of recognition pleased her so much that she involuntarily spoke the boy's name aloud. "Phillip Nolan."

She heard his gasp of surprise. "You don't know me." He whispered, and so did she.

"Of course I do."

"But we haven't seen each other in years."

"We never *saw* each other. I know your voice."

"But it's changed. I was only ten years old."

"A voice never changes when you're blind," she said.

Phillip Nolan went away. She heard him consulting with the other man and with the robot. She didn't know if Captain Clausen had heard her say the pirate's name, but she thought he was too far away. She decided to listen in on what the pirates were saying.

Phillip Nolan said, "No, she's sure, all right. I don't know how she does it, but you're not going to convince her that I'm not me."

"We have to." This was the second pirate, not the robot, the other man. "It's too soon for our identities to be known. If Matthew Carey finds out, he'll guess the rest."

"Then we have to prevent him from doing so," said the robot. She knew it was a robot now. Their voices were nothing like human ones.

"How? We can't kill her."

The robot said, "Of couse not, but we can take her with us."

"For how long?"

"For as long as we want. We can demand a ransom payment. The second man intervened. "I think that might work."

Nolan said, "We'll still have to let her go eventually."

"By then, it may not matter."

Alyc Carey could hardly restrain her glee. She cautiously reviewed every word the three had exchanged and came to the same conclusion: they were intending to kidnap her. The space pirates of Quicksilver. They still hadn't quite made up their minds. *Say yes,* she thought, *say yes.*

The second man made the final decision: "Then we'll do it that way."

Only Nolan remained uncertain. "She's the most vicious little thing in the Galaxy."

"Vicious?" said the robot.

"She'd as soon spit in somebody's face as talk to them."

"Then we'll spit back," said the second man. "You tell her, Phillip. Warn her to be good."

"Thanks," Nolan said drily.

Lady Alyc Carey waited tremulously for her name to be called. Kisha also seemed nervous, but Alyc was certain she didn't understand what was going on. Kisha could not hear whispering at such a great distance.

"Lady Alyc, could you come over here for a moment, please?"

It was Phillip Nolan. Alyc forced a reluctant Kisha to bring her forward.

Nolan leaned close and she could smell his breath. "I'm sorry you recognized me just now, but I know it'll do no good to try to convince you I'm not who I am."

"I knew you positively the moment you spoke."

"Yes, I understand that, but you must understand that it puts me—us—in a rather delicate position."

She did understand of course, and was willing to help ease his nervousness. "I'm sure you don't want your identity widely known."

"Then you'll promise to keep quiet?" He seemed eager to grasp at any alternative.

"My duty to the Emperor would prevent that." She kept a straight face, didn't even smile.

"Then I'm afraid we may have to inconvenience you even more than we have. We'll want to take you with us. It won't—"

Kisha made an angry snarl, and Alyc told her to be still. "I see that you have no alternative."

"Yes, that's right," said Nolan. "But you'll be treated well—I promise you. Our ship is as clean as any in the Empire and no one will bother you without your consent. We'll hold you for only a short time and then let you off at the first occupied planet we pass."

She knew he was lying but did not care. "That sounds fair enough."

"If you dare to harm the Lady Alyc Carey," Kisha hissed, "your bones will shatter in a thousand discorporation cells."

"She won't be harmed," Nolan insisted. "Just obey us—please,"

"I will," said Alyc.

His ordeal finished, Nolan asked Alyc and Kisha to stand by themselves. Then he went back to his companions and resumed collecting the passengers' loot. Kisha was weeping softly. "I knew I shouldn't have let you come. It is my fault. This is a terrible thing, and I am to blame."

Alyc was consoling. "We'll be all right, Kisha. That man is a noble. I know he'll treat us well enough."

"Your father will have me sent to the mines."

"I won't let him, and you know I won't. Now hush—there's no reason to cry."

Alyc could have cried herself—from joy.

Of course, it was sheer happenstance—good luck.

But she had won out. That was the important thing.

And this time it was for certain.

Alyc Carey had beaten the odds.

2 LORD TEDRIC

Once aboard their swift, sleek battletug, the *Vishnu*, the space pirates of Quicksilver wasted no time making a hasty getaway.

The pirates knew for certain that Captain Clausen of the *Oceania* had sent out a distress signal the moment the *Vishnu* had first approached. The chances were slim, of course, that they could be found and caught before many hours had passed. In N-space, physical matter does not exist, and finding any specific point in that gray vacuum is a tedious, time-consuming process. Still, on one other occasion, while attacking a bloated cargo liner, the pirates had been surprised by the sudden appearance of an imperial fleet cruiser only a few kilometers to the starboard. That time the *Vishnu*'s speed had saved their lives, but it was not a set of circumstances the pirates wished to repeat, especially now, with so much precious loot on board.

Within moments of the clanging of the airlocks, the *Vishnu* was on its way toward Quicksilver, the mysterious place the pirates claimed as home. Once they were free in N-space, no imperial vessel would likely ever catch them.

As the *Vishnu* raced away, five individuals were present in the tug's control room. If Melor Carey had been present, he would not likely have recognized any of them. His daughter, Lady Alyc, had already been escorted to the private room she would occupy for the duration of the voyage. If Matthew Carey had been present, however, he would most certainly have known at least three of those present and very possibly the other two as well. These five individuals represented the collective leadership of the space pirates. Two dozen men served under them in various capacities, but these other men were common criminals and renegades. Without the five in the control room, without their leadership, imagination, and dash, the space pirates of Quicksilver would never have flourished for a quarter of the time they already had.

The first of the five, as they stood in the room from left to right, was Alyc Carey's old boyhood companion, Phillip Nolan. Nolan was a slim man in his early twenties, with bright orange hair and chiseled, aristocratic features. Nolan wore a tattered silver uniform, the property of a lieutenant in the Imperial Corps of the One Hundred. His grandfather, Tompkins Nolan, whom Melor Carey would surely have recognized, had held command of the imperial fleet during the final, terrible years of the centuries-long war between the Empire of Man and the alien Wykzl. Even before that, the Nolan family had established a long, glorious tradition of imperial service. After the final defeat of the fleet, however, and Tompkins Nolan's subsequent disgrace, the family fortunes had taken a severe downward spin. Phillip was the youngest of three sons. He was a convicted mutineer, facing a sentence of death. Matthew Carey might have been angered to discover Phillip Nolan in the pirates' control room, but he would not have been surprised.

The presence of the second figure would not have surprised Matthew, either. This was a subman known as Keller, a former sailor in the imperial navy, recently sentenced, with Nolan, to die for the crime of mutiny. Keller was a small, furry individual, with a voice that hissed and growled. He spoke only when spoken to, but when he did, everyone listened.

Next came the two individuals Matthew Carey might not have recognized. The first of these wasn't a human being at all. He was tall, twice the height of Phillip Nolan, with a muff of blue fur circling his skull and a pair of twitching tendrils protruding from his forehead. This creature was a Wykzl, member of the first—and so far only—aggresive alien species encountered by mankind in its journey through the stars; his name was Ky-shan. Because Nolan and Keller were known to keep company with a Wykzl, the presence of such a creature would probably not have surprised Matthew Carey. The name Ky-shan

would have. Not because it held any special signifi-
cance but because, to Carey, all Wykzl looked pretty
much the same.

The most surprising figure present was certainly
the next, who sat at the control panel, operating the
tug. The only reason Carey might have recognized
this individual was because of his past notoriety. At
one time, when Carey was only a boy, there had been
no person more famous in the Empire. The name of
this figure, commonly, was Wilson. Officially, his
name was KT294578. He was a robot. And an outlaw.
For thirty common-years, Wilson (or KT294578), the
renegade robot, served as a scourge of the spacelanes.
He was accused of being a pirate, thief, smuggler,
murderer, looter, anarchist, and kidnapper. Some of
the charges were true. Seven common-years ago, with
a special squadron of corpsmen hot on his tail, Wilson
disappeared. He had finally been assumed dead, and
yet here he was again, piloting the command ship of
the space pirates of Quicksilver. (The *Vishnu* did, in
fact, belong to Wilson.)

The fifth and final figure, in turn, was another
person Matthew Carey would certainly have recognized.

He was tall, muscular, blond, as broad and powerful as a giant's fist. Like Nolan, he wore the silver
uniform of a Corps lieutenant and, also like Nolan, he
was an accused mutineer. Alyc Carey would have recognized his voice, because he had been the second
human present in the *Oceania*'s lounge. His name was

Tedric. Hardly anyone—including Carey—knew anything more about him than that. Tedric preferred it that way. He was a mystery man.

Tedric was presently speaking. He said, "I think if we can reach Quicksilver in an hour or two we won't run any risk of being spotted."

"I'll get you there in less than one," said Wilson, from the control panel. Like all modern robot models, KT294578 (Wilson) was built in close approximation to a human being. It would have taken a close inspection to tell that he was made from wire and plastic, not flesh and bone. He breathed, laughed, talked, and smiled. But he wasn't human; not one part of him. "We're home free. I promise you."

Keller, the mutinous sailor, moved away from the others and began fumbling through the crates of loot removed from the *Oceania*. "Look at all this. Money, money, money. Diamonds, rubies and emeralds. This has got to be our biggest haul yet."

"If we can convert it into credit," said Phillip Nolan, "which won't be all that easy."

"Not for us, maybe, but Wilson can do it. You can, can't you, Wilson?"

The robot nodded. "I've got my connections, sure. Trust this old robot. I haven't failed you yet, have I?"

"What do your connections say about Lady Alyc Carey?" asked Nolan.

Wilson grinned and turned around. "We ought to clear a cool million for her."

"At the least," put in Keller.

Nolan shook his head. "I wonder. None of you has met her. I have. If she's as mean with her father as she is with the rest of the universe, we might very well have to pay him to take her back."

"I think her father loves her," Tedric blurted out suddenly.

"Do you have any basis for saying that?" Wilson asked.

"It's just a feeling I had."

Wilson nodded. So did the others. All of them had long since learned never to argue with Tedric's feelings because, most times, they were right. The reason had to do with where Tedric came from. He wasn't born in the Empire of Man. He wasn't born in this universe at all. Tedric came from another sphere, from another place and time. The Scientists, mysterious inhabitants of the planet Prime, had used their powers to pluck Tedric out of his universe and bring him to this one. Tedric knew he was here for a purpose. He knew that purpose concerned the future fate and survival not only of the Empire of Man but of the entire human race. Other than that, he lacked any firm details. As a result, recently, Tedric had decided not to worry about what he didn't know.

And so he had become a space pirate.

That made sense, too. It made sense in terms of Tedric's life and experience to this time.

He had made his first public appearance within the boundaries of the Empire of Man some three common-years before when he arrived, mysteriously, at the artificial planet Nexus to attend the Imperial Academy of the Corps of the One Hundred. The Corps had been established during the most glorious years of the Empire, before the terrible war with the Wykzl. Originally true to its name—only the one hundred most qualified men in the Empire were granted commissions—the Corps had slowly decayed side-by-side with the Empire it served until, by Tedric's time, several thousand men held commissions and only a few ever actually stood active duty.

Tedric spent two years at the Academy. He excelled in his studies because of hard work and stood supreme at athletics because of natural ability. Phillip Nolan was a member of Tedric's class of cadets, and so was Matthew Carey.

A little more than one common-year ago, all three men received their commissions from the Academy. Each, for his own private purpose, chose to accept active duty. Nolan, as a third son, had little else to do. Carey, as his father's representative, felt the Corps would be a useful institution to control. And Tedric, as a stranger, chose as he did because—he then believed—the Scientists of Prime had told him to.

After graduation, all three men—along with the remainder of the class of cadets choosing active duty—received assignments to board the giant fleet cruiser, the *Eagleseye,* which was then about to depart for a planet known as Evron Eleven, where a rebel-

lion among the submen and subwomen laboring in
the Dalkanium mines beneath the planetary surface
threatened to disrupt the entire trading system of the
Empire. Dalkanium was a rare transuranic element
absolutely essential to the operation of the N-space
drive. Evron Eleven was one of the few sources for
Dalkanium within the Empire.

Phillip Nolan and Matthew Carey were rivals
since early childhood. The fate of their respective
families had followed oddly parallel courses. While
the Nolans declined, the Careys ascended. Tedric became close friends with Nolan. Again, he thought it
was because the Scientists had told him to.

When the *Eagleseye* reached Evron Eleven, Carey
—in command of the Corps contingent aboard the
ship—asked Tedric to lead the initial landing party to
the planetary surface and contact the rebellious min-
ers. Tedric selected two men to join his party. One
was Nolan and the other was a subman sailor, Assist-
ant Steward Third-Class Keller, who had once served
a term in the mines and thought his wife might still be
there.

The situation above Evron Eleven was further
complicated by the presence in orbit of a heavily
armed Wykzl battle cruiser. Since the end of the war a
century past, the Wykzl had largely kept to themselves. The reason for their presence here was a mystery. The Wykzl ship ignored all attempts by the *Eagleseye* to establish radio contact.

Tedric, Nolan, and Keller barely reached Evron

Eleven when they were captured and taken prisoner
by the rebels. Keller's wife, Jania, it turned out, was
one of the rebel leaders, although at first she refused
to acknowledge any relationship with the husband
who had deserted her. Jania took Tedric, Nolan, and
Keller on a tour of the deepest mines. What they saw
disturbed, disgusted, and angered them. Conditions
underground resembled a primitive hell. Tedric
came to understand the reasons for the workers' rebellion and to sympathize with their cause.

Before he could take any action as a result of
their findings, the Wykzl cruiser intervened by dropping a carefully aimed load of bombs upon the mines
and burying all the rebels, including Tedric, Nolan,
and Keller, kilometers underground.

With Jania's help, the three men managed to escape the trap. On the planetary surface, they stumbled across a small party of Wykzl sailors. After cap-
turing one of the aliens—Ky-shan—they stole a Wykzl
shuttle craft and managed to rendezvous in orbit with
the *Eagleseye*.

Aboard the ship, the first thing they learned was
that Matthew Carey had been tricked by the Wykzl
commander, Mo-leete, and taken prisoner aboard a
small lifeboat. The Wykzl were demanding the immediate withdrawal of the *Eagleseye* and the relinquish-
ment by Carey of his family's rights to the mines below. (The Dalkanium mines of Evron Eleven were
owned one hundred percent by old Melor Carey.)

While meeting with Captain Maillard of the *Ea-*

gleseye in the ship's control room, Tedric suddenly seized a sword, pressed it to the captain's throat, and demanded an immediate attack upon the Wykzl ship. Tedric believed he was acting under the Scientists' express orders, and he convinced Nolan and Keller to assist him in his mutiny. The attack was launched and, in the end, proved successful. Lured by the *Eagleseye* too close to an invisible black hole, the Wykzl cruiser disappeared with all individuals on board.

The victory of the *Eagleseye* erased, for the time being, any charges of mutiny against Tedric, Nolan, and Keller. Captain Maillard promised to lie to help their cause. Matthew Carey was rescued from the clutches of the surviving Wykzl, and Tedric, Nolan, Keller, and Captain Maillard journeyed down to the surface of Evron Eleven to accept the official surrender of the Wykzl commander, Mo-leete.

Mo-leete revealed to them the reason for his presence in imperial territory. He spoke of the sudden appearance within his stellar nation of a series of monstrous red clouds that expanded constantly, swallowing up entire star systems and those who inhabited them. The Wykzl required a steady source of Dalkanium in order to increase the size of their N-space fleet to combat these mysterious clouds. Mo-leete explained that his people had attempted to acquire the Dalkanium peaceably, but their request had been denied by Melor Carey. Direct action had thus seemed the only course left open to them and they had therefore attempted to take advantage of the workers' rebellion on Evron Eleven to seize the ore they required. They had failed this time—Mo-leete at least had failed—but others would come again. The survival of their nation and race lay at stake. Tedric, Nolan, Keller, and Captain Maillard each in turn promised to help the Wykzl obtain what they needed.

One further problem was Ky-shan, the Wykzl the corpsmen had captured during their escape from Evron Eleven. The Wykzl were a highly ritualistic species, and no ritual was more important to them than that of proper surrender. Because Ky-shan had been captured too quickly and never allowed the opportunity of completing the rite, he was now branded among them, fairly or not, as a coward and traitor. For him to return home would mean instant death, and for that reason Mo-leete left him with Tedric and the others. After some hesitation, they decided to accept their new companion and took him with them when they returned to the *Eagleseye*.

As the big cruiser turned in its course and headed toward Earth, where a reception led by the Emperor himself seemed certain, Tedric experienced a variety of confused feelings. He had believed all along that the Scientists had brought him to this universe for a specific purpose, but now he had to wonder exactly what that purpose could be. He reviewed his recent accomplishments and found nothing to equal the monumental tasks he sensed he must face.

Then he had a dream. At least, at first, he thought it was a dream. In this dream (or vision), his spirit left his body and flew through space to the planet Prime at the rim of the Galaxy. Here he spoke to one of the Scientists, who revealed to Tedric that he possessed certain unspecified powers of perception, and that it was these powers, not the Scientists themselves, that had guided his recent actions. Tedric was the master of his own destiny. He had been brought to this universe for a definite purpose, true, but he had been brought to lead, not follow. The Scientist also spoke of certain dark forces battling for control of the universe and hinted that the red clouds of the Wykzl had some connection with these forces.

Tedric returned to his own body determined to do what he could to serve the Scientists' purposes, even if he didn't know as yet what these purposes were.

But when he reached the Earth, it wasn't the Emperor who greeted him. It was a warden. Tedric, Nolan, and Keller were arrested on charges of mutiny in space. They were placed inside the imperial prison.

This was a period in his life Tedric knew he would never forget. Even buried in the mines of Evron Eleven, with tons of rock overhead, he had never felt so thoroughly defeated. He knew he couldn't blame Captain Maillard. He had surely done what he could. It was Matthew Carey who had had them imprisoned here. Tedric knew he would no more forgive Carey than he would forget the ordeal he faced.

The three of them were placed in a single cell deep beneath the streets of New Melbourne, Earth's imperial capital. The cell was a bare room, with thickly padded walls, ceiling, and floor. There were no visible means of entry or exit. A plastic case filled with pills of concentrated food sat in one corner. The supply seemed large enough to last several days, perhaps even a full week, if properly conserved. Tedric hoped such measures would not prove necessary. He fully intended to leave this prison as quickly as possible.

But Phillip Nolan laughed. "I'm sorry, Tedric, but I can't help myself. Sometimes I forget where you're from and that all of this doesn't make quite as much sense to you as it does to a native like me. How do you plan to pull off this act of departure? You're not going to escape, are you?"

"If it's necessary, I will. I assume it's not going to be."

"Then you're wrong—wrong twice." Nolan sat on the floor. It was soft and oddly comfortable. "First, the only way you'll leave this cell is if you escape and, second, there's no possible way you can ever escape from here. This isn't just a hole in the ground where they stick people who are nasty. This is the imperial prison. It was built a thousand years ago to house people like us who are considered evil beyond repair. No one has ever escaped from the imperial prison. I doubt that anyone has ever tried. It's impossible. Do you see a door? A window? Do you see any way bigger than a misroscopic dot that could ever get out of here?"

Ky-shan, the Wykzl, was also with them, but Ky-shan spoke only when spoken to, and right now, none of them was paying him much mind.

Tedric said, "Someone has to let us out of here eventually. For the trial, if nothing else."

Keller, who was leaning against a wall, said, "That's right, sir. They do have to give us a trial. It's the law. Once on a ship, I was accused of being a thief. The captain had to give me a trial, and I managed to convince him I was as innocent as a baby daisy."

"And were you?" said Nolan.

"What's it to you?"

"To me, nothing. To them, our unseen jailers, maybe a great deal. You see, Keller, we are guilty. We committed mutiny, and they know we did. We've had our trial. We've been accused, judged, convicted, and sentenced. It must have happened while we were still in space. If we weren't guilty, we'd never be here. They have that right. The law lets them, in certain extraordinary cases. I guess we're extraordinary. I don't have to tell you what the punishment for mutiny happens to be."

"Discorporation," Keller said bleakly.

"And that's just what can happen right here in this cell without us ever once seeing the light of day again. It might happen in nine seconds, nine days, or nine years. But it will happen. You can bet on that. If I were you, I'd be saying my prayers."

Tedric was thinking. "Then you agree that it wasn't Captain Maillard who had us arrested."

Nolan nodded. "I had my suspicions at first, sure, but not now. No, it wouldn't be him. I suspect he'd be here with us right now, except that the Careys have more use for him alive and obedient than dead and defiant."

"But there's no evidence against us. Even if Captain Maillard had talked, he would have done so after we landed, and we were arrested the moment we reached the Earth."

Nolan pursed his lips. "And that's what disturbs me the most. For them to lock us in here without any firm evidence means that someone is very angry with us indeed. But who?"

"Matthew Carey," Keller suggested.

"No, I don't think so. He's not powerful enough. It couldn't be him alone—it has to be old Melor himself. Whatever we did out on the edge of the Empire upset him so deeply that he's willing to twist the system to see us punished and dead."

"But what could it be?" Keller said.

"I just wish I knew. Logically, it doesn't make sense. We saved his mines for him. We made Matthew look like a fool, but I can't see that disturbing old Melor very much."

Tedric shook his head. "Phillip, I'm almost afraid the answer must be me."

"You, Tedric?" Nolan said softly. "No, I don't think that's true. The Careys hate me because of my family, but they barely know you. I doubt that Melor Carey could have heard of you at all."

"Could he?" Tedric shook his head. "I wonder."

"Is this another of your feelings?"

"I suppose it is. There's just something very familiar about that name: Melor Carey. I sense that he's deeply involved in this entire situation. I mean, the clouds, the Wykzl, everything. Remember, the clouds have never appeared inside the Empire. Why? The Wykzl think it's because we're inferior, but I can't accept that. Melor Carey is the most powerful single force in the Empire. He may not be a cause, but I sense that he knows who or what is."

"And he did refuse the Wykzl request for Dalkanium. They would have paid enough to make him rich, if he wasn't already. I assumed that was just his innate contrariness, his unwillingness to help an old enemy, but who knows?"

"Exactly, Phillip."

"But we have no proof. Only your feeling. That's not enough, Tedric."

"I agree, but . . . ." Tedric paused momentarily, searching for the right words to express his rather nebulous emotions. "Let me put it this way, Phillip. I was never afraid of Matthew Carey. I am afraid of Melor Carey. There has to be something to explain that difference."

Nolan nodded quietly. "Yes, but if there is, we'll never know, will we? Any moment now, we may all four be discorporated. It's a hell of a way to go, but there's no way out of here."

Despite this, no one seemed to be in a hurry to hasten their end. In the cell, where an unseen light source provided constant, dulling illumination, the only way of telling time was watching the rate of growth of Keller's beard. According to that rather approximate gauge, two days went by, perhaps three. Tedric, Nolan, Keller, and Ky-shan slept fitfully, ate sporadically, conversed occasionally. It was a truism that even the best company could grow tedious after an extended period together, and three days together in that tiny cell seemed like an extended period. That, and the continual tension of waiting, never knowing from one second to the next when their lives might be casually snuffed out.

A fourth day came and went. A fifth. Perhaps a sixth.

Then, all at once, the four prisoners fell asleep. It happened suddenly, as if they had been drugged.

When they awoke, they were no longer alone. A fifth person had entered the cell. This individual appeared to be a fully human male. He wore the torn rags of a beggar, and the exposed flesh on his face, arms, and chest showed a rash of red open sores. He wore a patchy beard and no shoes. He was neither obviously young nor old. When he grinned, his yellow teeth showed black gaps.

The man crouched in the corner of the room where the case of concentrated food rested. At the moment, he seemed to be shoving handfuls of that precious store down his throat.

Nolan rose up and shouted, "Hey, you! Get away from there!"

The beggar, grinning, went right on eating. "Got

to share your wealth," he said with difficulty, through
a full mouth.

"No, you don't." Nolan raced across the room
and attempted to grab the pills away from the beggar,
but the beggar reached out as casually as a man swat-
ting a bug and flicked his right hand. Nolan took the
force of the blow on his right shoulder and left his
feet at once. He sailed across the room and struck the
opposite wall. He bounced off and hit the floor.

"Ow," groaned Nolan.

Tedric approached the beggar more cautiously,
with a hand extended. "I really think you ought to
put those down. Our supply is limited and we don't
want to starve."

The beggar glanced up at Tedric and, at least for
a moment, ceased eating. "Starvation any worse than
discorporation? A dead man's a dead man."

"We prefer to wait." Tedric kept his hand
extended.

The beggar stared at Tedric's big hand, grinning, then finally gave his shoulders a casual toss. "All
right, friend. I'm not one to go contrary to another
man's convictions."

He held out the case of pills. Tedric accepted
them and said, "Thank you."

Still grinning, the beggar came swiftly to his feet.
He didn't lower his hand and now pointed it in Tedric's direction. "I'm called Stubb's, by the way. Very
pleased to make your personal acquaintance."

Tedric saw no way of avoiding the beggar's outstretched hand short of rudeness. So he shook. And felt immediately soiled. "I'm Tedric, and this is Phillip Nolan, Keller, and Ky-shan." He drew his hand back as quickly as he could. The stink of the beggar in this tiny cell was growing unbearable.

Nolan, who still lay stretched out on the padded floor, rubbed his shoulder. "I'm wondering if Stubbs here is even human."

"Hush," said Stubbs, with a conspiratorial wink. "That's supposed to be our little secret."

Tedric was willing to accept this as just another silly joke and return to his solitary contemplations. Boredom and isolation had sapped his energy to the point where he felt little curiosity about this new visitor. Another criminal, he assumed, doomed like themselves to eventual discorporation. Death was the great leveler. It made the quality of one's company seem very unimportant.

But then he had another of those feelings again, and he froze as he was.

Then he turned back to the man who called himself Stubbs.

At one time, during the first years after his arrival in this universe, Tedric had assumed these feelings were the result of the Scientists' tampering with his mind and memory, but they had denied this absolutely, and now he had to believe differently. The source for the feelings lay within. It was himself. Another organ of sensation, one not possessed by most other men, perhaps not by any other man. It wasn't telepathy. He didn't read thoughts. Nor was it, strictly speaking, premonition. He didn't know the future. What he seemed to sense was the truth of things, the raw facts that lay concealed behind the curtain of deceit and subterfuge.

He pointed a finger at Stubbs and said, "I don't believe you are human."

He had spoken with such certainty that there was a moment of stunned silence.

But Stubbs just grinned. He shook his head in admiration and said, "You are a damned quick one, aren't you?"

"But if he's not human," Nolan said to Tedric, "Then what is he?"

"He's . . ." Tedric began. He couldn't finish the thought. His feeling told him only what Stubbs wasn't, not what he was.

"Here, friend," Stubbs said to Nolan. "I'll answer that one myself."

And with that, reaching up, he removed his face.

Underneath lay another face, but this second one did not even remotely resemble the first. There were no lines and wrinkles, no open red sores or patchy beard. This second face was as smooth, clean, and scrubbed as a new born child.

"You're a robot," said Nolan.

Stubbs nodded. "You can call me KT294578."

"But what are you doing here?"

"Paying for my sins." The robot had not lost any of Stubbs. It was an incongruous attitude coming from that smooth face. "And recruiting," he added.

"Wait a minute." Nolan came off the floor at last. His expression showed that he guessed something deeper than anything yet revealed. "I know who you are."

"I told you my number," KT294578 said.

"But that's not how you're known, is it?" Nolan approached the robot, pointing a finger. "You've got a name, haven't you?"

"Stubbs?" the robot said tentatively and with amusement.

"No, not Stubbs. Try me again."

"You're pretty quick yourself." The robot grinned, showing Stubbs's yellow, dirty teeth. "Then, if Stubbs won't do, how about Wilson?"

Nolan stopped. It was clear this only confirmed what he had suspected all along, but the final revelation seemed to catch him by surprise. Even Tedric had heard tales of Wilson, the renegade robot, the scourge of the spacelanes. There was no more notorious criminal in the history of the Empire of Man.

"And everyone thought you were dead," Nolan said.

"Do I look it, friend?"

Nolan laughed and dropped down. "Not right now, maybe not, but how soon? You're in a discorporation cell. Have you forgotten? Whether you're Wilson or Stubbs, you're going to be dead soon enough."

Wilson laughed. Tedric couldn't recall hearing a robot laugh before. "Won't you give me a little credit, please? I'm in this cell because I want to be in this cell. You think a sly old robot like me would get himself caught after all these years? I told you I was recruiting, and that's the truth. I'm here to make you an offer. I want you as members of my outlaw band."

"I'd rather have something a little more permanent," said Nolan, glancing around the cell.

"Oh, bother that, man," said Wilson. "Do you think I'd come here voluntarily if I didn't know the best way out? Forget about dying for the time being, and let me have your undivided attention. I've made you my offer, and it still goes. I've got a fast ship and a competent crew to operate it. As you know, I've been away from the Empire for several years. Now that I'm back, I intend to resume my past activities."

"Which means killing and looting and stealing," said Nolan.

"It means I don't obey all the laws, yes," Wilson agreed. "But for you four it means not being dead. That's my offer in a nutshell. Serve with me and I'll save your lives."

"There's no way out of here alive," Nolan said flatly.

Wilson seemed to find that statement supremely amusing. He laughed, if possible, harder than ever. Finally controlling himself, he said, "Just give me your answer, then wait."

"Then of course we accept," Nolan said glibly.

Wilson frowned. "Hold on a moment, lad. Perhaps I have failed to speak with sufficient clarity. Accept my offer, and you're making an acceptance for life. This isn't one of your noblemen's party picnics."

Tedric, who had been listening intently to this entire conversation, intervened for the first time. He spoke quietly to Wilson. "Before I can promise anything for myself, I'd like you to answer at least one question."

Wilson nodded tightly. "Ask it."

"I'm not doubting the sincerity of your intentions," Tedric said, "but I can't help wondering. Why choose us? You say you broke in here to recruit us to your cause. Are we that important? You're taking a great risk coming here. This is the imperial prison and you are the Empire's most wanted criminal. What I need to know is why we're worth it. Surely there are other criminals not in prison and easily swayed to your side."

"There are fools, yes," Wilson said. "You see, Tedric, you have to understand that we live in an age of decadence. There are thousands of pickpockets, con men, and small-time thieves in this city, but those who are successful, those who are intelligent enough to make crime pay, have little interest in flying off with me to the distant stars. They're better off here in New Melbourne, and they know it. But you four—you're different. You're not criminals, you're outlaws, and outlaws are what I need to make my band thrive."

"I will not participate in wanton slaughter," Tedric said.

"Who's asking you to?" said Wilson.

"Then what exactly are you asking?"

"Nothing more than what I've always done. Steal from rich."

"And give to the poor," said Nolan, sardonically.

"And give to me. To us. From the Careys to the Nolans. I think that's fair."

"And you'll do it peaceably," Tedric put in.

"As peaceably as it can be done."

Tedric pretended to think, but he had really made up his mind. It was that special organ of sensation again, a private tickling feeling. He knew this was the correct thing to do. He told Wilson, "I'm with you."

"And me," said Nolan at once.

"And me," said Keller.

"And I," said Ky-shan, who had not previously appeared to hear a word spoken around him.

"Then welcome to the space pirates of Quicksilver," said Wilson, holding out his hand to all of them.

He still stank.

3 SPACE PIRATES OF QUICKSILVER

That decision—to go with the renegade robot Wilson and join his band of outlaws, rather than remain in the discorporation cell of the imperial prison and face certain death—was one Tedric never had cause to regret.

It was more than strictly a matter of survival, staying alive to fight another day. A feeling told Tedric that, since his first arrival in this universe, he had never accomplished anything as remotely worthwhile as what he was accomplishing with Wilson.

Worthwhile because it was directly connected with his aim in being here. By serving with Wilson, Tedric firmly believed, he was also helping bring about the eventual survival of the Empire of Man, the human race, and the universe as a whole. If he hadn't believed this, he would not have gone on. He did believe it, and he went on.

Even this very moment, in the control room of the speeding battletug *Vishnu* as it rushed through N-space toward the pirates' secret domain, Quicksilver, Tedric could not help recalling how it had been when he first made his decision to go with Wilson.

He remembered clearly the skepticism he had experienced when Wilson, pressed for the means by which he intended to escape the imperial prison, had reached into a pocket of the tattered beggar's trousers he wore and drew out five tiny pink pills.

"What are these supposed to do?" Nolan asked, with unconcealed suspiciousness.

"They'll save your lives," said Wilson.

"And how will they do that?"

"By killing you."

"Did you say kill?" said Nolan, drawing back.

"That's right, kill. As in death. The absence of life and breath. The cessation of all conscious experience."

Nolan laughed nervously. "And that's how you intend to free us from this prison?"

"It's well known," Wilson said, "that there's no way of escaping alive. So we're going to do it the other way: dead."

Nolan shook his head. "Wilson, you're beginning to make me wonder if everything I've been taught in my life is wrong."

Wilson looked confused. "I'm afraid I don't understand what you're talking about."

"I'm talking about the supposedly well-known

fact that no robot can go stark raving mad. I think you may be the first of your kind, Wilson."

Wilson laughed, and there appeared to be no hesitation in his glee.

Tedric decided to sit down to help ease the tension. He gestured at the others to do the same. "I do think Wilson owes us a bit more explanation than what we've received."

"It really isn't all that complex," said Wilson, sitting. "These pills are a most remarkable substance, and they really do kill you. Only it's not for good. Three common-hours, never more than four. I've ingested them a good hundred times, and you see me here now. I've been dead, and I've lived again."

Nolan said, "And what are our jailers going to think when they suddenly discover that we've died? If they do discover it, that is."

"Oh, they'll discover it, all right. Don't think just because you feel alone and isolated that every word you speak, every breath you take, every emotion you feel isn't being monitored and recorded. There's no such commodity as privacy in a prison. That's the first lesson every outlaw has to learn."

Nolan glanced nervously past a shoulder, as if expecting to see a flock of recording devices hovering nearby. "Then won't they know what we're saying now, our plans for escape?"

"They will, sure, but not right away. The computer that handles the monitoring isn't a bright boy. He's programmed only to jump when something extraordinary occurs in a cell. A softly spoken conversation like this isn't extraordinary. A fistfight might be or if one of you went nuts. When all five of us die, that'll be extraordinary."

"That does bring up another interesting matter," Nolan said. "Isn't this entire situation a bit too coincidental for comfort? How did you manage to get in here? How did you know for certain you'd be brought to this cell?"

Wilson's eyes gleamed with a peculiar delight. "I had assumed the answers to those questions were rather obvious. I had an accomplice, what do you think? Security here is too tight to expect to bribe a way out. But you can bribe a way in. That's what I did."

Tedric, leaning forward, pointed at Wilson's hand. "For myself, I'd like to get back to the matter of those pills. I still don't think you've told us very much about them. Just exactly how do they work? Nolan and I studied pharmacology at the Imperial Academy. I thought I was familiar with the effects of every drug known to man. I've never heard of any pills that can kill a person and then revive him."

"Who said this pill was known to man?" said Wilson, with his familiar grin in place.

Tedric frowned. "I'm afraid you're going to have to explain that, too."

"I got the pills from the Dynarx."

Ky-shan, whose expression and demeanor often seemed permanently frozen, bristled visibly at the mention of his people's ancient enemy. The fur on his back stood up straight. He snarled. "The heathen."

Wilson looked at Ky-shan and said, "The Wykzl here can tell you what I'm saying is true. The Dynarx use this drug as an integral part of their deepest religious rites."

"They are drug-crazed heathen," Ky-shan confirmed.

"He means yes," Wilson explained.

"I'm more interested in what you mean," Tedric said. "No human being has ever gone inside the Dynarx star systems and returned with his sanity intact."

"That's because those who stayed sane, stayed with the Dynarx. They didn't go home because they liked it where they were."

"And you didn't?"

Wilson shook his head. "It's a long story, filled with deeds of valor and betrayal, and someday maybe I'll tell it to you. For now, let me just say that the Corps was hot on my trail and the Empire of Man was no longer big enough to keep me hidden. I knew I had to get away, but where? So I threw the dice. They came up a certain way and that's the direction I took. I went to the Bioman Sphere first, but in spite of their vaunted superiority, they're really as dull as can be. I decided to try the Dynarx. I liked them, and they accepted me. When I decided it was time to come home, they bestowed a few gifts on me. These pills were among the gifts."

"So we have only your word," Nolan said, "these

pills are safe, that if we swallow one we won't be turned into frogs or worse."

"My word," said Wilson, "and your own paucity of viable options. You can stay here and die or die and go with me. I think, if you choose to die with me, I can guarantee your corpses will be better handled. What it comes down to is trust. Trust me or stay here. It's up to you."

Tedric held out his hand. "Give me one of the pills," he said.

"So soon?" said Nolan.

"We can't afford to wait," said Wilson. He handed out the pills, one each to Tedric, Nolan, Keller, and Ky-shan. He kept one pill for himself.

Tedric looked at the tablet in his palm. It seemed harmless enough, like a headache potion. This will kill me? he wondered. Then he swallowed the pill. Wilson was right. It was a matter of trust. Trust—and no options.

Nolan swallowed his pill.

Wilson swallowed his.

And Keller.

Only Ky-shan failed to move. He glared at the tablet in his big blue paw and said, "It is a breech of honor for me to touch the Dynarx blasphemy."

Tedric looked at him. "You won't go with us?"

Ky-shan seemed more sad than defiant. "I cannot."

"What if I order you to take that pill? I am your master. You failed to complete the rite of surrender."

Ky-shan folded his long arms across his chest and seemed to consider. "If you order me, I must," he said at last. "You are the master." He did not appear disappointed by this conclusion. Tedric thought Ky-shan was no more eager to die in this cell than any of them.

"Then I order you," said Tedric.

"And I obey." Ky-shan swallowed the pill and promptly resumed his stationary posture. He seemed unaffected by the act of blasphemy he had committed.

"How long until we die?" Tedric asked Wilson.

"Ten minutes, maybe twenty. A little longer for me, probably, since I ate so much just after I came. I apologize for my gluttony, by the way, but I knew we'd be leaving soon. I've been so busy the past three or four weeks preparing for our getaway that I didn't have time to eat."

Three or four weeks? Tedric wondered. "But we've only been here six days at the most," he told Wilson.

"You've been here," Wilson said, "for exactly thirty-six days."

Tedric shook his head, unwilling to believe, but there was no reason for Wilson to lie. Time could be a very funny commodity, Tedric realized. It was never certain and set. At different moments, for different people, it flowed in contradictory directions.

Tedric decided to concentrate on dying. What would it be like? The tips of his toes and fingers seemed already numb. Was that the beginning? His head felt light. If he stood, he thought he might fall.

A sudden thought came to him. He squinted, trying to observe Wilson seated on the floor across from him. "You spoke of having an accomplice." His words came slowly. "But haven't you implicated him? If our conversation is recorded, eventually someone will know about him."

Shaking his head, Wilson grinned. "You never asked me who my accomplice was."

"Then I'm asking you now."

"Guess."

"I—I can't," said Tedric.

Wilson winked. "My accomplice happens to be the same creature who reviews the recordings. It's the computer, Tedric, and that's how I know we're home free. We machines stick together. When I approached him, the computer was glad to help—for a price."

Tedric smiled. "You're a very intelligent robot, Wilson."

"I've had to be. For a hundred years, I've been an outlaw in a realm where illegality is supposedly impossible. I have to be as quick as lightning. It's the only reason I'm alive

"You'll be dead soon."

Wilson winked. "But only for a while."

That was when Tedric died.

Death is the most personal and private of all conscious experiences, and even afterward Tedric never found himself able to discuss what occurred to him in the imperial prison that day. Death was an experience that all of them shared, yet none ever spoke of it later. Not Nolan or Keller or Ky-shan or even Wilson, who knew it best. Each one died alone and for four common-hours, as the universe swayed obliviously past, they remained dead, but death was a place beyond description as surely as life was an experience created from words, and there was no way they could speak of what they had known, even if they had wished. Tedric never forgot one moment of those four common-hours. He never forgot, but he never thought of it. Death was beyond thinking too.

When he awoke, Tedric was alive and lay in darkness. Resurrection was a sudden process, not like the slow, painful emergence from sleep. One second, he was dead, and the next, he lived again.

He raised his hands as far above his body as they would go. A heavy weight stopped them. Tedric pushed against the weight but it did not budge.

Cautiously, he surveyed his situation. I am lying in a box, he decided. There was a soft cushion beneath him and a pillow for his head.

I am in a coffin, he decided.

In all of man's long history, few things had changed less than the ritual of death. Tedric knew he would not be buried underground. He would be burned, discorporated. But words would be spoken first. Words that looked back to man's superstitious past: *There is death in life, life in death.* What did the ancients know of the great insoluable mystery of life and death? More than they might even have guessed, Tedric now knew.

But he wasn't dead. He lived again.

So, putting his trust in Wilson, he waited to be freed from the coffin of his death.

The light, when it came, struck his eyes a savage blow. He cried out, blinking, and waved his fists at the yellow empty air.

When he finally could see, a face hung suspended above him. A grinning face.

Wilson.

"How did you like it?"

"Being dead?" Tedric said.

"What else?"

"I am alive now?"

"Of course you are."

Tedric sat up in his coffin. "Then where are we?" Looking around, he could see a dim, tiny room containing, scattered across the concrete floor, five steel boxes, one nearly twice as long as the others. Ky-shan, thought Tedric. Two of the boxes had their lids pried open, while the other three remained sealed. The room smelled very sweetly of overly ripened fruit.

"This is the prison's funeral parlor," Wilson said.

"Then we're still not safe."

"My accomplice made sure we were brought here. He's not ambulatory, so he can help us no further."

"You do have a plan?"

"I know the way out."

Tedric climbed out of the coffin. With Wilson's help, he unsealed the other three and released Nolan, Ky-shan, and Keller. All were awake, alive, and alert. They were very subdued, unable to speak above a whisper. Ky-shan shook uncontrollably, as if from the cold. It was hot in the parlor.

Wilson reached into the pockets of his tattered trousers and pulled out a pair of matching miniature heatguns. The weapons were powerful enough to stun a man, if not kill him. He handed one weapon to Tedric and kept the other. "My accomplice made sure these were planted inside my coffin. I hope they won't be needed, but if they are, at least we'll be ready." With a wink, Wilson went to the door, opened it easily, glanced out, turned back, and wiggled a finger. "You folks ready?"

No one seemed hesitant. For himself, Tedric was more than eager to leave this place. The sense of death that hung about the room gave him shivers.

The four of them bustled out after Wilson.

The corridor beyond was narrow, straight, and poorly lighted. Wilson led the way, his gun extended in front of him, his bare feet squishing against the padded carpet. Tedric went to the back and trained his weapon upon the darkness behind.

For perhaps ten minutes, they moved in a straight line. Now and then, they passed another corridor branching off perpendicularly from the one they followed, but Wilson seemed to know exactly where he was going. They passed a number of doors along the corridor, some of which showed a line of yellow light underneath. Once, Tedric heard voices. He held his gun tighter until he had moved safely past the door, but nothing happened.

At one of the branching corridors, Wilson swerved suddenly to the left. The others followed compliantly. This corridor was darker than the first, and the floor, damp with seeping moisture, was not padded. The air smelled of disuse. Tedric moved cautiously. His footsteps clicked, setting off a spasm of echoes. He peered into the gloom at his back. Were they being followed? He knew, even if they were, he would not have known. There was a temptation to fire off a round of shots to be sure. He resisted the impulse. That would be foolish, he knew. But it was a different world down here, dark and mysterious. He had barely had time to glimpse the massive glass and steel city that lay overhead. Now it no longer seemed to exist.

Wilson stopped. Nolan, Keller, Ky-shan, and Tedric did the same. Tedric could hardly see past the Wykzl's huge shoulders. He heard Wilson say, "Tedric, I need your help."

Tedric squeezed past Ky-shan and went forward to join Wilson.

There was a broad square steel plate set in the wall. "We have to get past this," Wilson said.

"What is it?"

"The entrance to a ventilation shaft."

"That's how we're going to escape?"

"Yes, and I don't think I can budge it. The KT robot series was not built for physical strength."

Tedric reached up and tried to get a grip on the steel plate. It lay flat against the wall and seemed unmovable. The light was very bad here, and he had to squint to see at all.

"Any luck?" Wilson said.

"Let me try again." Tedric was already perspiring and his breath came quickly. Finally, with much tugging, twisting, jerking, and pulling, he managed to slip the fingers of one hand under the edge of the plate. Then, bracing himself, he gave a fierce jerk. The plate groaned, giving slightly. Tedric jerked again. The plate gave more. He could fit his whole hand under it now. He jerked a third time. The plate came off in his hand.

And a blast of cold air slapped his face. He sniffed at the gap in the wall. The odor was strong, unidentifiable, not pleasant.

"In we go," said Wilson.

"What's at the other end?"

"You'll see."

"What if we're followed?"

"We can't be—not for long. The ventilation system is like a maze. I'm the only one who knows the right path."

"Then you'd better go first."

"I intend to."

Tedric looked at the open shaft. It did seem large

enough to hold a crawling man, but only just large enough. "This was your plan? To escape through here?"

"It's worked so far, hasn't it? The worst is behind us. The computer may be the only one who remembers this system exists."

But that wasn't what Tedric meant. He had been wondering about something else. "What if I'd refused to join you? Then what were you going to do? You said yourself you couldn't budge the steel plate."

Wilson shrugged casually. "Life is full of risks and gambles. Here, we can't stand talking all day and night. Give me a hand."

Tedric linked his fingers and boosted Wilson up toward the open shaft. After Wilson had slithered inside, Tedric helped Nolan and Keller follow. Kyshan, tall enough to reach the opening without assistance, went fourth.

Tedric came last.

Inside the shaft, Tedric hunched his shoulders and used his elbows to move. Progress was worse than a crawl—it was a slither. For the longest time, Tedric could still see the dim rectangle behind that showed the place where they had entered the shaft. Any pursuers, stumbling across the open hole and peeping through, would have them trapped. Tedric kept a tight grip on his gun. The cold air continued to rush past. The odor he had noticed before was worse than ever in here. He tried to breathe through his mouth. The shaft turned at a slight angle. Now he couldn't see the opening anymore. He didn't know if that made him feel better or worse. He slithered past a number of other shafts branching off from the one Wilson continued to follow.

None of them spoke as they crawled. Tedric could hear the heavy, labored breathing of the others as they struggled to edge forward. He did not like buried places like this. He was too much reminded of the time on Evron Eleven, deep in the mines, when for a few moments, he had believed himself to be buried forever alive. This place was no better. There was the constant blast of cold air and the sickly sweet scent that went with it, worse than any imagined death. And he wasn't his own guide. Wilson, leading the procession like an unseen god, held onto his future fate with cold mechanical hands. With Ky-shan slithering in front of him, Tedric could see nothing beyond the black bulk of the alien's hindquarters. On Evron Eleven, he had once observed the creatures who worked the bottom layers of the mine. They were things, no longer even faintly human, with dark pits for eyes and huge shovel-like hands. Am I becoming one of them? he wondered. Tedric could no longer glimpse his own hands. He crawled on.

At last, after an indeterminate period, he heard a sound that might have been Wilson's cool voice: "I think we've reached the end."

Ky-shan stopped ahead. Tedric bumped into him. "What do we do?" he called. His voice boomed like a drum. He could not control it.

"We're going out. Be careful. I'll go first."

That much seemed obvious. Tedric tried to be

patient. He counted from one to fifty and started back down again. He heard another distant sound that might have been made by bare feet striking a hard floor. He swiveled his head, trying to peer past the alien in front of him. He saw something there. Something bright. A light?

"I'm out." This time he recognized Wilson for certain. "Okay—next."

Tedric was the last to go free. The ventilation shaft came to a sudden end, dropping into emptiness. Tedric thrust his head and shoulders into the vacant air. There was a circle of light, but it moved up and down like a puppet on a string and blinded his eyes. He decided to tumble out. One foot caught on a raised surface at the mouth of the shaft. He hung in the air. Big hands wrestled him loose. He turned upside down and stood on wobbly knees.

The blinding light turned out to be a lantern held in a man's hand.

Nolan thumped Tedric on the back. "We made it! We made it! Saved from the jaws of death!"

Tedric tried to laugh, but it wasn't funny. Not until this moment had he realized that for a long time he had truly expected to die.

There were people crowding all around, strangers. They were short, oily, ragged people. Some of them smelled, but the worst odor came from the place itself. They stood on the floor of a broad round concrete tunnel. Scattered pools of water, some as deep as twenty centimeters, exuded the sweet stench that pervaded the air shaft. Tedric still couldn't see well, and the crush of strange friendly bodies sent him splashing through the unseen puddles.

Wilson was suddenly beside him, shaking his hand. "I told you I had a plan, didn't I? Now look at this. Everything worked out perfectly."

As dazed as he felt, Tedric managed a rational question. "Where are we?"

"Haven't you guessed? No, I suppose you haven't. Look, do you know what a sewer is? We're in the sewers of Old Melbourne."

Tedric knew what a sewer was: a system of underground tunnels used to carry urban waste. That explained the odor. "You mean they still exist?"

"You're in them, friend." Wilson put an arm around Tedric's shoulders. "Come on, let's get out of the wet."

All of them—including the crowd of strangers—turned away down the tunnel. Wilson splashed through filthy water and Tedric stuck close to him. They came to an iron door in the side of the tunnel and Wilson went through it. There was a tiny room filled with giant rusting machinery. Wilson sat down on the flat surface of a machine and beckoned at Tedric to sit with him. A dozen people filed through after them. Someone hung a lantern on a hook. Tedric looked around and saw Nolan, Keller, and Kyshan. The door was closed. The room was crowded.

Wilson stood up, waving his arms for silence. When he got it, after a brief interval, he said, "Ladies and gentlemen of the underworld, I just wanted to thank you for saving the lives of my good friends here." Tedric saw that Wilson was right. A close inspection revealed that more than half the strangers gathered here were ladies—or women at least. In the Empire of Man, where women were normally treated like fragile glassware, this was a peculiar sight indeed. Wilson began to point. "I want to introduce you to my companions. Here beside me is Tedric, the traitor. Over there, to your left, Nolan, the renegade. Beside him, Keller, the mutineer. And, finally, the tall fellow, that's Ky-shan, the rogue Wykzl. While they're among you, I can only hope they'll be treated with the same benevolent kindness you've shown me. Words fail to express the depths of their humble gratitude."

That seemed to be the end of Wilson's speech. He jumped down from his perch and took Tedric's hand. "Now it's your turn to meet some of them."

What followed was a confusing whirl of names and titles. A few Tedric did not immediately forget. He remembered Milo, the pickpocket king; Sharma, the jewel thief; and Regina, the mad poetess. All of these people were fully human. Wilson explained in a whisper as he led Tedric through the mob: "This is the cream of New Melbourne's criminality. There are hundreds of others scattered through the sewers, but only the best are permitted to rub shoulders with a famous outlaw like myself. They helped plan our little escape. I think you owe them a debt of gratitude."

"I thought you'd already taken care of that for me—in your speech."

Wilson laughed. "So I did." His voice again dropped to a whisper. "When I first came here, I had hoped to build a crew from among them, but hardly anyone nowadays is eager to follow a spacerat like me to the stars. You can't really blame them. Their life's good. They've got a good system. When civilization is busily collapsing, the pickings are ripe for any criminal with halfway quick hands."

As Wilson spoke, his voice rose. A woman standing nearby—Tedric thought she was the one introduced as Regina, the mad poetess—came closer and said, "Being a criminal is better than holding an occupational code. That's why we admire Wilson so much. He not only discarded a code, he got rid of his entire identity as a robot."

"I'm the robot who refuses to be robotic," Wilson said, with a wink.

"We think of him as our patron saint," Regina said.

Wilson showed no embarrassment at such praise. His skin, artificial or not, seemed to glow. Tedric left him in Regina's company and crossed the room to where Phillip Nolan stood alone.

"Isn't this amazing?" he said.

Nolan nodded solemnly. As the child of noble parents, he seemed disturbed by so much outlawry. "It's almost like a second world down here. I lived in New Melbourne for years and never knew about this."

"You knew there were criminals?"

"Oh, sure, but not this many—not this organization. It's really incredible when you think about it."

Wilson had joined them again. He winked in Nolan's direction and said, "And pretty damn tempting, too, right?"

"Well, that's not exactly what I meant," said Nolan.

"What you meant was that space is in your blood the same as it's in mine. The pickings are easier here on old Earth but bigger up there. Getting rich is something any fool can pull off—your pal Carey is proof of that. You and I are aware of what's really worthwhile."

Before Tedric could ask Wilson to explain what was really worthwhile, the door behind them opened and two women crowded into the room, bearing a wooden crate. When the box was opened, it disgorged a stream of bottles of excellent wine, which were quickly uncorked and passed from hand to eager hand. Everyone drank. After a few minutes, Wilson began to sing. His voice—a raw quavering tenor —was a revelation. Tedric didn't know any of the songs but he hummed along with every chorus. When the song was sad, there were tears in his eyes. When the song was happy, he smiled. When the song was obscene—as more than several were—he blushed. Nolan was singing, too. He had his arm around one of the women—was it Regina, the mad poetess, again? —and at the end of every stanza, sad or happy or dirty, he gave her a puckish kiss on her soiled cheek. Ky-shan was drinking wine. He didn't sing, just drank.

The party continued, long, loud, and raucous, through the night—or was it day? Tedric had never drunk wine or any other intoxicant during the life he could remember, so it wasn't long before shapes began to blur and waver before his eyes, and his knees, when he tried to stand, wobbled and shook like sticks of straw. Everything suddenly seemed incredibly funny to him. Even Wilson's raunchiest songs were hilarious now. Ky-shan, when he fell asleep on his feet and toppled to the floor upon two unsuspecting outlaw ladies, was screamingly funny. Nolan, when he stood up and staged an impromptu dance upon the edge of one of the big machines, culminating in a two-meter sommersault to the crowded floor below, was hilariously funny. Everything was funny. Everything anyone said, did, mumbled, or performed was funny. Warm, sweet, delicious, delightful, funny. Then Tedric fell asleep. It was a sleep like no other he had ever experienced—dreamless, dark, warm, sweet, and very funny.

When he awoke in the little room with bodies carelessly strewn about in various stages of dress and undress, nothing seemed funny. The air was full of the bitter stench of stale wine. Tedric grabbed his head, then reached desperately for his stomach. He didn't know whether to moan, weep, scream, or just be sick. The inside of his mouth tasted as though birds had slept in it.

A big hand dropped upon his shoulder. "About time. I had intended for us to be two hundred miles up in orbit by now."

Tedric lifted his head and blinked fiercely. The shape of the hand on his shoulder showed clearly enough but the face looming beyond was faint, splotched, distorted. He guessed its actual identity more from the familiar voice than any visual evidence. "Wilson," he said.

"Well, it's not the Emperor of the Universe, of that much I'm sure."

Tedric continued to blink. He could see Wilson's face now, as bright, beaming, and cheerful as ever. He couldn't stiffle a moan. Life seemed suddenly unfair. Wilson had drunk more wine than any other four people combined. "You said something about orbit?" said Tedric, with a fuzzy tongue and parched lips.

"While you were soundly sleeping, a couple of the ladies and I surreptitiously rented a shuttle from the port. My own ship is in orbit right now, and I'm a bit eager to reach her. This town has gone hot for the five of us. Do you realize we're the first creatures ever to escape the imperial prison? I don't want to hang around long enough for the inspectors to get a clear scent. Even the underworld isn't impenetrable."

"And you intend to leave Earth today?"

Wilson looked at the timepiece implanted in his left wrist. "In exactly seven minutes. Better rouse the others."

Wilson removed his hand, and Tedric took that as a signal he ought to try to stand. He made it as far as his knees before the swimming in his head got the best of him and he had to pause to catch his breath. By now his sense organs spoke to him more clearly than before. He was aware of the steady melody of rhythmic snores that filled the room from a dozen separate mouths. And he could see faces on some of the slumbering bodies. There was Nolan, Keller, and Ky-shan. Always before, the Wykzl had slept on his feet, if he slept at all. His big, blue, furry body seemed quite at home among the various shades of pink, brown, black, and yellow flesh.

"You could have warned me, couldn't you?" Tedric said, gripping his skull in his hands.

Wilson laughed. "It's hard to warn somebody about something you don't know from personal experience."

"You mean you don't get intoxicated?"

"Didn't you see me last night? Sure, I do, but for a robot it doesn't have to be permanent. If I don't feel like waking up the next morning with a big head—not that a robot ever sleeps—I just empty my veins and let the contaminated blood run out. It means I'm immobilized for a half-hour or so while my body cooks up a new supply, but among friends that's no danger, and I only drink with friends." Wilson showed Tedric his right wrist, where a thicket of healed gashes could be seen. "But enough chatter. Let's be off. Here, I'll give you a hand."

Wilson gripped Tedric's arm and drew him to his feet. For a long delirious moment, Tedric wavered, then he took a tentative stumble ahead. His knees worked; his feet moved. He decided, eventually, that everything would be okay.

While Wilson went to make final preparations for their departure, Tedric busied himself trying to rouse

Nolan, Keller, and Ky-shan. With none of Wilson's gruff insistence at his disposal, Tedric found the task far from an easy one. Still, at the end of twenty minutes, he stood among a moaning, groaning, whining, sighing company of two pale men and one trembling Wykzl.

Wilson came back to say it was time to go.

The journey through the sewers to the spaceport proved uneventful. Several of the underworld outlaws went with them. They left the sewers at the edge of the port and proceeded cautiously to the place where Wilson's surreptitiously rented shuttle waited.

Before boarding the craft, Wilson delivered a brief speech of farewell. He spoke of friendships formed in a brief time and of the warmth and gratitude he personally felt. The listening outlaws applauded politely. Wilson turned and opened the shuttle door. Nolan rushed suddenly away and darted into the crowd of outlaws. He grabbed one lady, embraced her warmly, and kissed her lips. Tedric could not be sure, but he thought it was Regina, the mad poetess, again.

The shuttle received clearing instructions from the tower. Tedric was amazed at how easily all of this was carried out. Billions of people throughout the Empire obeyed the law. If they had only known how easily evaded those strictures could be, he wondered how long it would take the outlaw population to exceed the law-abiding.

The shuttle took off through the air.

Wilson put them into orbit, then set about

searching for his orbiting craft. From the outside, when it was found, the ship looked like any ordinary battletug, but from within there was something odd and alien about the sharp, clean angles of the rooms. Tedric felt suddenly ill-at-ease.

Wilson explained. "This tug is the *Vishnu*. I named it myself, but its true origin is in the Bioman sphere. I stole the tug from them when I left."

Tedric thought that explained his feeling of unease. "Is it any different from an imperial tug?"

Wilson grinned. "Well, for one thing, it can travel faster than light."

"No," Tedric said, in wonder.

"You bet. How else did you think I was going to get us from Earth to my headquarters on Quicksilver? This little tug is equipped with an N-space drive. I'll have us home inside of a week."

A tug of this size capable of such velocities was utterly beyond the technological capabilities of the Empire. From Ky-shan's astonished expression, Tedric guessed the same must be true of the Wykzl. No one had ever doubted that the Biomen, mutant humans created by the radioactive firestorm of humankind's final civil war, were the most technologically advanced of the four known interstellar species. There was little firm proof, however. The Biomen for centuries had refused any contact with their parent race, the men of Earth.

"Have you inspected the engine to see how it works?" asked Tedric.

"I've tried, but there's no way. The Biomen seal

them up tight when they build them and I haven't found the tools yet to break that seal."

"But what if the engine malfunctions? There has to be a way of making repairs."

"The engine hasn't malfunctioned as long as I've had it. I doubt that it ever will."

"But everything wears out. It's a natural law—entropy."

"The Biomen don't recognize that law."

"That's absurd."

"Not for them." Wilson shook his head. "Unless you've lived among them, as I have, you can't possibly know."

Tedric had to accept Wilson at his word. Of the trillion residents of the Empire of Man, Wilson alone could speak with authority of the Biomen. Still, Tedric was not unaware of the strategic importance of a ship such as this. If the Empire could somehow force the ship to divulge the secrets of its technology, such knowledge would provide an incredible leap forward that might well make a second war with the Wykzl, a conflict Tedric believed was inevitable, a far more equal contest than the first. Tedric imagined that Kyshan was aware of this, too, but there was really no point in considering the question now. At the present moment, the Empire of Man was the Empire of Melor Carey and his family, and Tedric would do everything possible to prevent their private power from growing any larger.

As the *Vishnu* sped through N-space toward its

mysterious destination of Quicksilver, Wilson took time to explain what he had in mind once they arrived. "Now that I've finally got a crew I can trust, I don't intend to hesitate another day before setting to work. I've marked out a list of a half-dozen planets worth hitting. You'll be especially pleased, Nolan. At the beginning, I'm limiting my targets to Carey holdings. Since they're the richest bunch around, they're the ones who can afford to lose the most."

The morality of space piracy still gave Tedric several uncomfortable moments, but he had already made up his mind to approach Wilson regarding a certain proposition. The robot had spoken only of acquiring wealth for his own pocketbook. Tedric thought that was a severely limited view. He had something much more complex in mind, and he thought that Wilson, who did not lack imagination, might well agree. Still, that was something that would have to wait until later. Tedric wanted to get a look at this mysterious base, Quicksilver, before proceeding further with his own intentions.

He never did get a look at Quicksilver.

That's because it could not be seen.

The *Vishnu* dropped out of N-space and approached the brilliant orb of a white dwarf star. The instrument panel confirmed the presence of one E-size planet in orbit. The *Vishnu* moved toward that planet. Tedric turned to the viewscreen to glimpse this world, his apparent new home, and saw nothing but the blackness of the void.

He looked back at the panel: the planet was only a few hundred thousand kilometers away.

He looked at the screen: nothing.

The panel: yes.

The screen: no.

The *Vishnu* began to drop down and through the porthole Tedric glimpsed a sudden rush of white clouds.

"Where did it come from?" he finally cried.

Wilson was laughing. Nolan, Keller, and Ky-shan were no less surprised and confused than Tedric.

"That's my secret," Wilson was saying. "Have you ever heard of a better pirate base? An invisible planet, a world as big and round as the Earth itself. They'll never find us here because they'll never see us."

"It shows up on the instruments," Tedric said. The *Vishnu* was already braking. He glanced quickly out at a green, brown flat world.

"On ours," said Wilson, "but not theirs."

"This is a Bioman device, too?"

Wilson nodded. "The secret of invisibility. I stole it from them."

"But it's not possible to—"

Wilson put his fingers to his lips. "I warned you never to say that when you're talking about our ancient cousins. With them, everything is possible. This is Quicksilver planet and you can't see it. What more evidence do you need than your own eyes?"

Tedric shook his head. Once again there was nothing he could say.

The space pirates of Quicksilver had arrived.

4 STONE CASTLE

Once the *Vishnu* safely reached the invisible world Quicksilver with its booty of kidnapped prisoners, Tedric went immediately to the private room he occupied in the upper reaches of the big stone castle that stood beside the side lake.

Wilson had always insisted that he had built the castle himself soon after establishing his headquarters on this out-of-the-way world, but Tedric found that claim hard to believe. It wasn't only the size of the castle, the complexity of its design. There was too much of an air of mystery about the castle, an atmosphere lurking in its bare rooms, twisting staircases, and windy corridors that could come only from great age. The castle made Tedric think of the creations of some once grand and proud race, now utterly vanished, obliterated by time, so that only this one big castle and its air of ancient mystery still testified that such a people had ever existed. And there was something painfully familiar about the castle, too. It wasn't one of his famous feelings—this was different. It was almost as if he had lived in such a place before, not here in this universe, but rather long before, in that other world, in the forgotten home where he had been born. The Scientists had confessed that, when they'd first brought him here from that other universe, an unforeseen effect of the displacement through time and space had been to blot out any conscious memories he might have possessed of a previous life. Still, despite this, things sometimes came back to him, most often in dreams at night. He saw stark visions of a cold, bleak stern land. One with castles? Perhaps—yes, perhaps. That was all he could say. And the familiarity of the castle never went away.

Because he had known her before, Phillip Nolan was chosen by Wilson to lead Lady Alyc Carey to the room that would serve as her cell. Before they separated, Tedric had asked Nolan to come to his room as soon as he was through with the prisoner and now he sat patiently waiting for the familiar fist to come knocking at his door. The room Tedric occupied was only sparsely furnished. Although there was a bed, he often chose to sleep on the stone floor. More often than not, he wasn't home. Since their arrival here from Earth, Wilson in his insatiable lust to rip the Empire again and again had allowed no one any rest. The *Vishnu* had struck a dozen backworld planets and five liners in a few brief common-months. The castle was stuffed with loot. Lady Alyc Carey was only the latest addition.

As soon as he heard Nolan's knock, Tedric hurried to open the door. A rush of cold air accompanied Nolan, threatening to extinguish the oil lantern Tedric kept on a wooden table. "Here, look at this," cried Nolan, pointing at his own face. His left cheek showed a series of red welts. "She scratched me when I went to lock the door."

"Lady Alyc?" said Tedric, surprised.

"No, that vixen with her. That subwoman. She's as nasty as an alley cat."

"Maybe that's her ancestoral genes."

Nolan shook his head. "More likely a tiger."

The two men squatted upon the floor, facing each other. Despite the obvious disparity in their backgrounds—Nolan third son of the Empire's most distinguished family—Tedric the nameless stranger from an alien universe—the months they had spent with one another had forged a deep bond of friendship that allowed them to sit like this for hours at a time without either feeling the need to chatter. Not only that, but when they did speak, the words they used often seemed to form a private telegraphic language, where the antecedants lay well concealed from the prying ears of eavesdropping strangers.

"I think the time's come to talk to him," said Tedric.

"Because of her."

"It complicates matters, to be sure, and also endangers our own position. I just don't think we can wait any longer. I never minded being a thief, but kidnapping is different."

"You weren't opposed while we were on the ship."

"And I'm still not. But we have to talk to him. We have to explain what we have in mind."

"I'm not eager." Nolan made a deliberate shiver. "I'll admit he scares me."

"But we can't wait."

"No."

"Then you're ready?"

"I suppose so. The worse he can do is hang us as mutineers. I've already faced discorporation over that once."

"Then let's go see him now."

"All right."

But they didn't move at once. For several more moments, the two men sat in mutual silence, each with his private thoughts. Then, as if by prearranged signal, they stood. Tedric grabbed the lantern off the table. Nolan opened the door. They stepped into the windy corridor.

A stone staircase awaited them. Tedric turned to his right and began to ascend the broad steps. The castle contained more than a hundred rooms. Of these, barely a dozen were presently occupied. They passed one where a light shined under the door: Keller's room. Farther up the staircase, there was another light.

"That's where I put her," said Nolan.

"I hope it's comfortable."

"In this place?" He laughed.

"I rather enjoy it here," Tedric said.

At the summit of the staircase stood another room where a crease of illumination could be seen. Tedric stopped, raised his fist, and knocked firmly.

"Come in, men," said a voice through the door. It was Wilson.

Tedric and Nolan stepped inside.

This room was twice the size of the one Tedric occupied but far less roomy. Crates and boxes heaped with money, loot, and jewels filled every conceivable meter. Wilson sat crosslegged in the center of all these riches. He winked at Nolan and said, "Something happen to your face, friend?"

"Lady Alyc's subwoman scratched me."

Wilson laughed. "Now, if you were me, you could put on a new face."

"Well, I'm not you."

"Sit down, men."

Tedric looked around for an empty place and finally found a secure nook on top of a sealed crate. Nolan joined him there.

"We've come to make you a proposition," Tedric said.

"We have a plan," said Nolan.

"We want to speak to you about this." With a wave, Tedric indicated the crates and boxes surrounding them.

Wilson's eyes immediately narrowed with suspicion. "You want to share. You don't trust an old robot."

"No, that's not it at all." Despite the many times he had rehearsed this conversation, Tedric couldn't help squirming under Wilson's cold, unhuman eyes. No matter how closely he resembled a man, Wilson never quite succeeded in concealing his mechanical heritage.

"Do you want to spend it?" Wilson asked.

Tedric nodded. "In a way, yes."

"In what way?"

Tedric saw no choice but to deliver the set line he had long ago memorized: "I want to use it—and us—to seize control of the government of the Empire of Man."

Wilson didn't laugh or wink or make a face, all of which surprised Tedric. Instead, he looked solemn, almost worried. "I think you ought to explain that a bit more deeply."

Tedric nodded, as pleased as he was amazed by Wilson's reaction. "I don't know about you, but I've seen it on every backworld we've visited. The Empire no longer exists out here. It's a name, no more than that, held together by nothing stronger than tradition and loyalty and the fact that there's nothing around to take its place. There's supposed to be an imperial navy and a Corps of the One Hundred, but we all know how weak they are. In all our raiding and piracy, what sort of obstacle have they presented?"

"Little," said Wilson, "or none."

Tedric nodded. "The only real reigns of power out here in the edges of the Empire are those held by the Careys and other corporate families. You can't tell me the settlers feel any devotion to them. The Careys do nothing but exploit. They reduce the submen to the level of slaves and use the fully humans only as tools for their own personal gain. Phillip and I saw what the situation was like in the mines of Evron Eleven, and I can't believe it's any better elsewhere."

"Nobody ever said it was," said Wilson. "But so what? Life is brief and ugly. It usually has been. What are you and I supposed to do to change that?"

"My feeling is that we have to find a worthwhile use for the loot we've collected. Remember how Nolan once made a joke about taking from the rich and giving to the poor and how, when he said that, you laughed and said you were more interested in taking from the rich and giving to yourself. Well, I'm saying the smart thing is to have it both ways. We take from the rich, as we have, but we give to the poor, as Nolan suggested. If we do that, in the end, I think we'll be the ones to gain overall."

"And that's your best suggestion?" Wilson said.

Tedric refused to back down in the face of the robot's implied derision. "I think it'll work."

"And what will Carey do all this time? We've stolen from him, and he's stood for that, because he's too rich to go broke because of a few pirates. If we try to take his Empire away, he'll be a lot less agreeable."

"Agreeable or not, no one man is all-powerful. We've seen the strength of the navy and the Corps.

Nothing they have—nothing Carey has—can match the *Vishnu*."

"Nothing we've seen so far, you mean. Carey has half a hundred ships at his disposal. We have one."

"But we have—or can have—one thing he doesn't: the loyalty of the backworld planets."

"By taking from the rich and giving to the poor."

"Yes."

"I wish it were so easy."

"I never said it was. I said it was worth trying, and that's all."

"Why—"

The question startled Tedric, who had expected almost anything but that. "Huh?"

"Why should we do it? What's in it for us?"

"The possibility of helping to bring about a new Empire of Man uncontaminated by things like the Carey family."

"And I should worry about the Empire?"

"You live in it, don't you?"

"In it, yes, but not of it. Don't tell me you've forgotten again already: I'm not a man; I'm a robot."

"But you were made by men. Don't you owe—?"

"No," Wilson said sharply. "I owe nothing to anyone."

"Then you won't let us do it," Tedric said, sensing defeat.

Wilson shook his head. "I didn't say that. You see, there's one thing you've neglected to tell me. You haven't mentioned the Scientists, Tedric."

This time Tedric was more than startled: he was shocked. "You know about the Scientists?"

Wilson nodded. "I know about them, and I know about you: who you are, what you are, how you came here."

"But you can't possibly—"

"They told me. The Scientists did."

"You've met them?"

Wilson nodded sadly. "On Prime. It was my mistake."

"I think this time it's you who owes an explanation," Tedric said.

Nolan's eyes were as filled with surprise as Tedric's, though for different reasons. Despite their close friendship, Nolan had never fully accepted Tedric's story of his secret meetings with the Scientists. Now that tale was being confirmed by the most rational of all living creatures, a robot. Nolan knew about the Scientists. They were supposed to be a group of utterly brilliant human beings who had long ago severed relations with the rest of the human race in order to follow their own peculiar destiny. The Scientists lived on the planet Prime at the edge of the Galaxy, where they observed the relentless doings of their distant descendants with a mixture of pride, irritation, and benign indifference.

"As you know," Wilson said, "I recently spent several years away from the Empire. When people ask, I explain that I left because the Corps was hot on my trail, but the Corps was no more apt to catch me then than it is now, which is to say I had few worries. I went away because I'd lived a long time and was sick of what I was doing and tired of what I was seeing. I wanted to go places and do things no living creature had ever done before. I went to the Bioman sphere. I lived among the Dynarx. Even then, I wasn't satisfied. All my life, I had heard about the mysterious Scientists and their sacred planet at the edge of the Galaxy. I asked the Biomen about them and was told they did not exist. I asked the Dynarx and was told how to find Prime. So I went there."

"And they didn't turn you away?" asked Tedric.

"That's what I had expected too, but, no, they did not. Regrettably, they let me in. I thought I'd pulled off a keen trick, but I was dead wrong. I'd come to Prime for reasons of my own—call it curiosity, if that's what you want—but the Scientists had let me land for purposes of their own. They took me in, gave me shelter, answered my questions. Even that last part did me little good, though, because neither a fool nor a wise man will ever learn much from life till he discovers the right questions to ask, and on Prime I was like an ignorant babe. Then, when I ran out of questions, the Scientists started telling me the things they wanted me to know. They told me about you, Tedric."

"Me?"

"Sure. What do you think? It was an accident I came to Earth just in time to set you free and bring you here? Hell, I halfway wish it had been. I wish that, because for me the whole idea of accidents has ceased to have much meaning. The Scientists told me there was a man named Tedric, who was the most important single individual in all of creation, and I was supposed to help him. You think I stole the *Vishnu* from the Biomen. I told you that because it made sense and because it could be one of their ships. But I never stole anything from them. The Scientists gave me that ship, and they gave me the secret of invisibility. They said, here take this and get back to the Empire and save Tedric and let him have his way. They never once said what the whole thing was about, but I didn't hesitate. I knew they were playing me like a puppet on a string, but I didn't dare tell them no."

Tedric well understood Wilson's feelings, because he had shared so many of them. A puppet on a string. He had felt that way himself. "Why haven't you told us this before?"

"You never asked, did you?" Wilson grinned. "Look, I'll be blunt, saving the universe really isn't my cup of tea. I'm plenty content to be what I've always been, a dirty outlaw, a renegade robot. I knew who you were and I'd push things hard on my own. But now I see it's too late. You've come to me with this proposition. I've either got to help you or refuse you. I just wish I could believe, whichever I decide, it's all my own judgment."

"The Scientists aren't here now," Tedric said.

"Are you sure?" Wilson kept grinning, but it was clear he wasn't amused. "You see, that's what bothers me the most. Just how far back does all this go? How deep? All the time I was on Prime, I got the feeling

nothing was an isolated incident. My life hasn't been a
normal one. I'm something that's not even supposed
to exist, a renegade robot, when I'm programmed to
do what I'm told. How come? Was it my choice? Was
it faulty programming? Short circuit? Or was it maybe
the Scientists all along? I can't answer that, but I don't
like even having to ask it. The illusion of free will is
damn important to me. When you're man's creation,
a machine designed to appear human, it's a struggle
to maintain any firm identity. The Scientists can take
that away from me, and I don't like it."

"Then you won't help?" said Tedric, attempting
to find some firm meaning amid the robot's
ramblings.

"Yesterday, no," Wilson admitted. "I'd had
plenty of time to think it out, and that was my decision. I knew this paradise wasn't going to last, that
eventually you were going to get restless and want to
save the universe, but I figured I'd done enough to
help. I wouldn't hinder you, keep you from leaving,
but the *Vishnu* was mine and I'd recruit another
crew."

"You said that was yesterday," put in Nolan.

"On the ship, I intercepted a message."

"Oh."

Wilson reached into the pocket of his vest and
drew out a sheet of folded paper. He tossed the paper
toward Nolan. "Read it for yourself."

Nolan read the message, then passed it to Tedric.
"That's hard to believe," he said.

Emperor Kane IV dead in palace New Melbourne,

Earth, read the first line of the transcribed message.

"You're not doubting it?" said Wilson.

Nolan shook his head. "He wasn't that old."

"What about the crown prince, Randow?" asked Tedric, who had by now also read the second line of the message.

"There's no mention of him at all."

"In prison?"

"It seems likely, yes."

Emperor Matthew I (Carey) to be coronated six common-days subsequent funeral, read the second line.

"And that's why I'm with you," Wilson went on. He thrust out a hand suddenly, wanting to shake. "I'm with you and the Scientists and the great rebellion against the crown. I've got an iron stomach, but this is too much even for that."

Tedric shook Wilson's hand. Nolan, in turn, did as well.

Wilson said, "And there's also a very important and strategic consideration. The backworlders might very well have hesitated to raise a hand against kindly old Kane IV. They'll feel none of that loyalty toward a Carey with a crown on his head. There's an old saying that revolution consists of nothing more than a bunch of angry men stepping forward and kicking down a rotten door. If this doesn't qualify as a rotten door, then I don't know what does." Wilson crossed his arms upon his chest. "So when do we start?"

Tedric showed his confusion. "But I never thought . . ."

Wilson laughed. "I know. You never thought I'd

say yes. Well, as I explained, that wasn't a half-blind guess till yesterday. Are you open to suggestions?"

Tedric still couldn't think clearly past his surprise. "Well, yes, of course."

"Because," Wilson said, "my suggestion is that we start tomorrow. By now, this message has been received all over the Empire. People will be damned angry. I suggest we move before they have time to cool off. And there's one other item we shouldn't forget."

"What?" asked Tedric.

Wilson grinned. "The Emperor's sister. Let's never forget we have the Lady Alyc locked away in a back room."

5 THE BLACK BEAST

Aboard his private shuttle the *Blue Eagle* less than half the distance between Milrod and earth, Melor Carey chewed his nails and grinded his teeth because the pace was too damned slow.

Short of a liner or cruiser, a shuttle like this, basically a miniature N-space drive with a bubble cockpit at its snout, was the one way of traveling between the stars at a velocity faster than light. The trip between Milrod and Earth would take only fifteen common-days, but even that was too slow for Melor. Damn it, he thought, how can I control a situation when I'm not even there? The situation existed on Earth; Melor Carey existed in space. That was the one thing in life he could not bear: waiting.

Matthew, his son, was on Earth, but Melor did not trust Matthew. Matthew was a product of his own genes, and Melor fervently believed in the inexorable deterioration of the genetic line. A great father could not produce a great son. His belief lacked scientific justification, but it was no less powerful for that. What it meant was stress: his own finite lifespan laid a limit on his personal achievements. What it meant was that throughout his life he had known he had to hurry. And this shuttle would not do that. It poked between the stars, while on Earth the situation reached a critical juncture.

He had already once violated his own stern beliefs, when he had allowed Matthew to go to Evron Eleven rather than finding some excuse for making the trip himself. There, the two men Tedric and Phillip Nolan had emerged to salvage the situation for reasons he had never fully deduced, but he believed that was Matthew's fault, too. If Melor had been there himself, outside intervention would not have been necessary, and another new force would not have emerged to challenge his own control of the Empire.

He did not fear Tedric and Nolan now. Wherever they were, wherever they'd gone after their unprecedented escape from the imperial prison, they presented no apparent threat. It was the situation itself that disturbed him, the way it refused to develop in accordance with his own long held designs. Matthew did not know the full nature of those designs. Only one man did: Melor himself. And he was not the sort who chose to confide in an object so tenuous as his only son.

The shuttle was the smallest—and thus the quickest—that had ever been built. Melor Carey rode in the cramped cockpit with a single companion: a robot technician, programmed for dexterity, who handled the entire complex of control panels. One of the few good things about robots was that they never talked until they were spoken to, and Melor Carey had not uttered a word during the seven-day duration of the trip. Right now, he sat in a tiny chair at the rear of the cockpit and watched, without real interest, as the robot moved swiftly through his programmed paces.

He blamed the damned Emperor. The former Emperor. The deceased Kane IV, whom Melor had met personally twice in his life. He tried to picture the man. Old. That was the one impression he always formed when he thought of Emperor Kane: old, even though Kane's birthday actually dated some two years following Melor's own. It was a classic example of genetic deterioration. More than a thousand years of absolute rule by a single family line. Melor knew his imperial history as keenly as anyone. He knew about Shorter II, who had written the imperial code, and about Terran the Great, who had led a fleet of warships into Wykzl territory and emerged victorious after obliterating five planets. He never questioned the strength of past emperors, but he knew Kane IV, and he knew the crown prince, and he knew what genetic deterioration could do in one thousand years to transform brilliance into stupidity.

Kane IV had assumed the throne after his grandfather's abdication at the end of the Wykzl war. Carey had met with him then, and when Kane—looking old even that early—had begged for his support as the Empire's last great hero, Melor had promised to do what he could. And he had. Within a half-dozen years from the date of his promise, Melor Carey stood as the Empire's most powerful man, and the Emperor himself had been reduced to a role not so much as puppet but of statue. Melor had never hated the man. He hated only what he feared, and there was no reason to fear an Emperor who, his spies told him, spent his days reading books, reciting old poetry, and listening to ancient musical tapes. The spies described Kane as a quiet, soft-spoken, kindly man, generally willing to treat his friends and enemies with equal diffidence. They also said, sometimes late at night the Emperor would rise from his bed and go to an open window and stand there for hours at a time and weep, softly, quietly, without end. Melor never liked that part. It didn't make sense, it didn't fit his picture of the man, and that disturbed him. It seemed to hint at the presence of a deeper well hidden away beneath Kane's shallow shell, but nothing had ever come of it. The Emperor just went on weeping.

And now he was dead.

The lack of warning had enraged Melor. It seemed totally unfair. He recalled the exact moment when he had first received word. He was sitting in his back garden on Milrod Eleven, sipping a cool detoxicant, attended by silent robots and bustling submen, when the paper appeared in his hand. At first he assumed it was another letter from Alyc about the dullness of her voyage through the stars, but then he saw it came from Earth, and he read quickly:

KANE DEAD. INCREDIBLE BUT DEFINITE. RAN-DOW IN A WILD TIZZY. ANY SUGGESTIONS? DE-TAILS WILL FOLLOW. MATTHEW.

It was the details that soon followed that enraged him the most.

All his life, he had never for an instant doubted that Kane would precede him to the death cell. In his plans, he had envisioned a slow death for the old Emperor, with much sadness and ceremony, capped at the end by a sworn declaration, easily forced from the hand of a dying man, where his proper successor would be named. It hadn't worked out that way. One moment Kane was alive, and the next he was dead. The written declaration now existed, of course, but it was a forgery. Melor Carey was a careful man who preferred to lie and cheat in the most honest possible way.

SUICIDE, said Matthew's second message. He went on to explain how the Emperor had cut his throat from ear to ear, never hesitating one moment, a straight, clean, and certain wound.

Why? Melor Carey wondered, but he forced him-self to shake his head. He refused to consider the maze of possible motivations; facts were all that mat-tered. He guessed, in spite of himself, that the suicide must be connected with Kane's inexplicable crying fits. The old man had left only one paper at his death, a terse few lines indicating his wish that his son, Randow, succeed him. That paper had been destroyed and the forgery substituted for it. Would that be enough? Would that alone salvage a measure of order from the chaos Kane had caused? He didn't know. He wasn't there. He wouldn't be there for another eight common-days.

Bitterly, Melor slammed his fist against the chair behind him. "Hurry," he cried. "Hurry this damn thing and get us going."

The robot pilot turned from his controls and said calmly, "Our present velocity represents the peak N-space performance of this craft."

"Then exceed it," said Melor.

"I am not programmed."

"Do it anyway."

"The master jests," said the robot, with a mocking smile.

"The hell if I do." Melor stood up and turned away. He would go to his room, try to create a calming environment there. The room, a few square meters with an iron cot and toilet, lay directly behind the cockpit. Melor first checked his private radio channel to be sure he had missed nothing during his absence, but the console was bare. Involuntarily, in disappointment, he reached for the transmitter but resisted the temptation. To call Earth again now, when there was nothing he could say or do, would only broadcast his own impatient fear. He couldn't let that sort of weakness be glimpsed—not even by his own son.

So he went to bed instead, struggling to reach the low mattress. The refusal of his body to perform the most casual physical tasks irritated him. It was too clear an indication of his own age. Melor was well past one hundred years, certainly nothing exceptional for a fully human being in this interstellar age but old enough to begin to experience the first signs of real aging. He didn't mind growing old; he hated being reminded of death. Not that he feared it. Melor feared nothing he could not touch, see, hear, or smell. If anything, when it came, he would welcome death. But not now—not too soon. When he finished his plans, then he would die, not one day before. It wasn't fair of his body to remind him constantly that death was one of the few things in existence he could not totally control.

He lay that way, with his eyes shut and his body tense, thinking of age and death, when the nearby voice spoke.

It said, harshly, "Melor."

He knew at once who it had to be. He opened his eyes. The blasted thing stood before him.

It was the black beast.

"How—how did you come here?"

The beast laughed deeply. "I represent those who would speak with you, Melor."

This was the answer the beast always gave. Angrily, Melor said, "I know who the hell you are. What I asked was—"

He tried to sit up. That was a mistake. Because of the limited size of the room, the bed occupied a cramped corner where the ceiling slanted sharply down. Melor, rising up quickly, struck his forehead against the ceiling. The blow stunned him. He reached up, grabbed his head, and cried out. The beast chuckled, like a child viewing a hurt man and unable to comprehend the pain.

Melor spluttered, like a young fool himself: "Damn you—you—"

"I represent those who would speak with you," the beast said again.

Melor wondered: was the damn thing mocking him?

He said, "Then speak, damn you, speak." He had recovered from the shock of his hurt sufficiently so that he could again see the black beast clearly. He struggled to meet its unwavering gaze.

Melor called the thing the black beast because that was what it looked like. The first time it had appeared before him—the first of what was now several dozen occasions—it had told him its name. He had long since forgotten those nonsensical syllables, but the image of the beast remained. What was a name? It was the beast that mattered.

It resembled a beast, too. A coat of black fur covered its humanoid body from toes to neck, but the face, except for patches of slick black skin on each cheek, was a tumult of rainbow colors. Two yellow fangs protruded from between thin lips. The only garment the beast wore was a fluffy white silk collar around its neck. The eyes were narrow, tiny pink slits.

The beast stood as high as the room—as high as any room, Melor realized, for it was shorter here than he remembered from the last time—and spoke in a guttural growling voice. The first time the beast had appeared to him, Melor had assumed it belonged to some breed of subman, but that was a mistaken impression. The beast was no man. It was alien. Even now, Melor did not know who it was, where it came from, or what it represented when it spoke. In the past, he had obeyed its utterances. The beast had told him to win a battle, seize an empire, control a human race. It had told him what to do and how. Melor had obeyed. The most recent time, the beast had appeared to tell him how to protect his mines on Evron Eleven. That time, what it said had been wrong—for the first time.

Melor could not forget that error. He glared at the beast. "I did as you said. I sent Matthew to Evron Eleven with the *Eagleseye*. I nearly lost my mines to the Wykzl."

The beast appeared undisturbed. "That was ordained."

"What do you mean? Do you mean you wanted me to lose those mines?"

"I desire nothing. I am an agent of others."

"Then what about them? Is that what they wanted?"

"I cannot speak of them—only for them."

Melor chuckled. "Then you were wrong—they were wrong. I kept the mines."

"There was a miscalculation," the beast admitted.

"Then get out." Melor waved at the door, as if the beast should go that way. "I've heard enough to convince me. First, you steered me wrong. You've always been on my side before, but now I can see you're no guardian angel. Second, you were wrong—you miscalculated. If I'm going to receive and accept advice from mysterious things that materialize out of thin air, that advice damn well better be infallible."

"Be silent, Melor."

"Then you better tell me why—and quick."

"Motivations are not your concern, Melor—or mine."

"Then get out. I'm through with you. I made up my mind the last time what to say if you came to me again. Now go."

Melor had never doubted the reality of the black beast. An ordinary man, confronted by such a specter, would most likely have regarded it as a product of one of three sources: madness, dreams, drugs. But Melor knew he wasn't mad, never dreamed, and refused all drugs. The beast was real because he saw, heard, smelled—a sweet perfumey stench—and, had he wished, touched it.

The beast smiled coldly. "I will go when I have told you what those I represent wish you to know."

Melor pointed at the door and used his firmest tone. "I said to go now." He knew it was useless. As real as it might be, the beast lay far beyond the power of human command.

"Listen, Melor, listen," said the beast, lowering its

voice to a bare whisper. "You journey now to the imperial capital with a set purpose in mind. Those I represent have surveyed all that has been, all that is now, and all that soon must be. It is their wish—and my command—that you immediately desist in your purpose. Matthew Carey, your son, shall not sit upon the imperial throne. Prince Randow must reign. This must be done."

Melor could not have been more surprised if the beast had demanded his suicide. He resisted the impulse to refuse at once. His whole life, the totality of the grand design, had been aimed at making the imperial family the Carey family. The beast knew this. He had revealed his hopes and fears often enough in the past.

"That is absolutely impossible," he said.

"But it must be done."

"Why?"

"The reasons are not yours to determine," said the beast. Was that anger flashing in its eyes? "You are commanded and must obey."

"The last time you came to me with a command, it proved to be a mistake."

"A miscalculation," the beast corrected. "I warned you of the danger of the man called Tedric. Unfortunately, he proved to be even more powerful than we feared."

"I had him imprisoned on your advice. I had him sentenced to die."

"But he escaped."

"Oh, you know that, too."

"Those I represent know everything," the beast said calmly.

But Melor was no longer so sure. "They mean nothing to me. I'm a free man. There's nothing to make me do what you say."

The beast showed its anger clearly. Melor had never seen it like this before, and he had to admit that he was frightened. "If you fail to do as you are commanded," said the beast, "those I represent shall not be amused. A violent curse will be placed upon your head. You must obey my commands."

Melor shook his head slowly. He refused to let the beast overwhelm him. "Then you're going to have to explain what went wrong out around Evron Eleven. I obeyed you then. Instead of going myself, I sent Matthew, and he nearly ruined everything."

"That is true from your limited perspective. Those I represent see much farther."

"How far? I nearly lost my mines to the Wykzl. Are you saying that is not important?"

"Important, perhaps, but not critical. The purpose of the expedition was less to protect your mines and more to determine the true nature of certain contrary forces now at work in the Empire."

"Contrary? Contrary to what?"

"To the will of those I represent."

"You're talking about this man Tedric, I assume. But what is he? Nothing but a common Corpsman. He doesn't even have a family name."

"But he is a threat—a terrible threat."

"And because of him Matthew cannot become

Emperor?"

The beast flared again. "You must never question me regarding the motives of those I serve. You
must only obey."

"But I. . ."

It was too late. The beast, smiling thinly, vanished as suddenly as it had appeared.

Melor fell back on the cot and wiped at his face.

A perfume sweet stench hung in the air.

Matthew shall not be the Emperor, he thought.
The beast had so commanded.

Trembling, he held his head. He couldn't wait. It
had come down to this. The moment was near at
hand. Matthew must assume the throne at once.

But the beast said otherwise, and he had never
disobeyed the beast before. What should he do?

For the remaining days it took for the shuttle to
reach the Earth, Melor Carey never once emerged
from the sanctuary of his own room. He spoke to no
one. He ignored the radio. For eight days, he quietly
considered what he knew must be the most crucial
decision of his life. Should he obey the beast, as he
always had, or should he simply ignore its command?

When the shuttle reached the spaceport on New
Melbourne, Melor Carey disembarked carrying a single battered valise. His son, Matthew, dressed in the
silver uniform of a lieutenant in the Corps of the One
Hundred, greeted him. "Sir, I have some terrible
news. I tried to contact the shuttle, but the radio
semed—"

"I know, I know." Melor held up a distracted

hand. He and Matthew walked side-by-side. "I didn't answer the radio. I was busy—thinking. Something came up." In his present state of mind, no news could possibly be described as terrible. He had met the black beast and heard its command.

Matthew went on, "It's the space pirates of Quicksilver. I just received word myself a short time ago. They've captured a liner."

Melor shook his head. The pirates had captured many liners. So what?

"It was the *Oceania*," Matthew said. "They boarded her, and . . . and they took her away."

"Took who away?" Melor stopped, took his son by the shirtfront, and squeezed. That name meant something to him. He knew the *Oceania*.

"The pirates have kidnapped Alyc."

Melor released Matthew. All at once, his whole body trembled. "Yes, yes, yes," he murmured aloud. "The bastards. They must have known. They must have seen."

If those the black beast represented were truly omnipotent, they must have known what would happen to Alyc. They could have told him, warned him.

They had said nothing.

Melor Carey had made up his mind.

"Father, are you all right?" said Matthew. "Shall I call a medical technician?"

"I—no. I'm fine." Melor took Matthew's hand and led him toward the waiting terminal. "We must hurry. That's our only problem. We must proceed without delay."

"Proceed with what, sir?"

"Why, with your coronation, of course. With your coronation as our new emperor."

Melor let the words stun Matthew as the two men walked together. He thought how easily they had come. Without forethought. Without agony.

He had dared to disobey the beast and what it represented.

He looked at the sky. The clouds did not open. Lightning failed to strike.

But now what? thought Melor Carey as he accompanied his son, the future Emperor, across the slick dark pavement of the port.

6 NARABIA

In the beginning, long before the creation of the Empire of Man, the invention of the N-space drive affected the most significant alteration in the consciousness of the human race since the day men first learned to fly. This moment in time—more accurately a period of several centuries—is known to historians as the Great Scattering. Before the Scattering, the human race knew nothing beyond its home world and a handful of barren planets and dusty satellites congregated near the warmth of a single ordinary stars. Quite suddenly, the human race became aware that this one star could be transformed into a thousand and those few planets, many tens of thousands. A close analogy would be with a blind man abruptly able to see for the first time in his life. At first, the formerly blind man staggers around in circles, unable to comprehend the sensory bombardment of sudden sight. Soon enough, however, the formerly blind man is moving, tentatively exploring his new world. Then he is luxuriating in it. Then, finally, he is merely a part of it, and an outside observer can no longer separate him from any other normally sighted man.

The Great Scattering proceeded in a similar fashion. At first, told that it could reach the star, mankind did little or nothing. The exploring teams eventually came next, pioneers who visited the planets of distant stars and returned to tell what they had seen. Mass colonization followed. In the first few years, hundreds left the Earth and its sister planets. Then there were thousands. And, finally, more than a hundred years after the invention of the drive, more than ten million men and women each year went to the stars to live. The last stage, complete integration, came with the founding of the Empire of Man. By then, it was quite impossible for an observer to say whether a man was born and raised on Earth or had never known anything except the stars.

The Biomen, of course, went the farthest. They set up their own nation and soon ceased all intercourse with the Earth itself. The submen went where they were told, and their story is less one of Scattering than of scattered.

But what of the fully human beings who went to the stars? Was it true that they were no different from those who elected to remain behind?

Tedric knew there was a difference. It was internal, not on the surface, where it could be spotted by an observer, but it existed nonetheless. At the Acad-

emy, studying old books, he had learned of this difference, and now, as he traveled between the backworlds accompanied by his friends, the space pirates
of Quicksilver, he confirmed through his own senses
the existence of this difference.

The men who colonized the stars were men who
had thoughts of their own. They were rebels. Political, religious, social, philosophical rebels. Perhaps not
consciously—and very rarely outwardly—but rebels.
The vastness of the Galaxy offered a multitude of
empty planets where a man—or group of men—
could think, live, and act in accordance with his own
personal terms.

A nation of fishermen made obsolete on Earth by
the death of the great seas could journey to another
world and there find oceans as deep and plentiful as
any ever imagined.

A nation of herdsmen doomed to extinction by
the efficacy of concentrated foodstuffs could uncover
a new planet where the grass grew as tall as a grown
man's chest.

At the Academy, Tedric had learned of these
backworld settlers and the planets they inhabited.
Now, he had come to Narabia, the lone planet of a
young white sun, whose inhabitants descended from
a nation whose homeland on Earth had long ago been
buried underneath the glittering glass-and-steel tow-
ers of a city of a hundred million. On Narabia, the
nomads roamed an empty planet, a vast blasted desert such as the one that had long succored their dis-

tant Terran ancestors. It was a world where they could live in the fashion they wished, undisturbed by the presence of strangers.

On Narabia, the pirates followed the same pattern used on the other worlds they had visited. The first thing they did was bestow gifts garnered from their accumulation of loot. Then, in the afterglow of the gift-giving, they conferred with the political leaders of the planet, seeking their help. On Narabia, this step proved especially difficult, for the planet was populated by more than one thousand tribes whose contact was limited at best. In order to achieve their aims, the pirates were forced to visit as many of these tribes as possible.

To travel from place to place, Wilson revealed a heavier-than-air prop-chopper which, if nothing else, at least amazed the technology deprived natives. Each tribe had one leader known as the Darkal. In most instances, the Darkal was also the oldest man in the village. The pirates soon learned that on Narabia an old man might be no more than a boy—sixty or fewer years. Life on the desert world was harsh, brutal, swift, and brief. The natives seemed to wish for nothing more.

This was the tenth tribe they had visited so far. The Darkal, seated across the tent with a toothless grin in the center of his yellow-brown face, appeared nearly as old as the Empire itself, but when he spoke, his words showed good sense, considerable knowledge, and great learning. Tedric had already learned not to patronize these backworld leaders. It was possible to be a wise man without ever glimpsing the sun of the Earth.

Inside the tent, with a brutal wind whipping outside, a dozen men sat in a circle around the electric fire. Only the pirate leaders had undertaken this expedition; the remaining men, petty criminals and youthful adventurers, had remained at home on Quicksilver. Nolan spoke for the pirates. Wilson and Tedric were also present. Ky-shan and Keller remained with the prop-chopper. As wise as some of them might be, the inhabitants of Narabia might nonetheless be disturbed by the sight of a subman or an alien Wykzl.

"We received news of the coronation of the new Emperor," said the Darkal, "and were disturbed. Still, what occurs on Earth rarely affects us, for we are a busy people. There is little time to worry of such matters."

"But you are citizens of the Empire," Nolan said. This was a tactic agreed on by all of them. In past meetings, it had become obvious that most backworld people took great pride in their imperial status. Many had served in the navy. Nearly all had a father or uncle or brother killed in the Wykzl war.

"We are full and equal citizens with any of you," the Darkal said. The men seated to his left and right, all of them elders, nodded in sage agreement. "My own beloved father shed the blood of his life in the war against the blue aliens."

Nolan nodded, as though impressed by this revelation. "Then through his blood, if nothing else, you owe your loyalties to the true emperor, and this man, Matthew, as I have explained, is a rank imposter."

The Darkal shook his head slowly. "This is mere politics." A bright ruby ring glittered on his left index finger, a gift from the pirates.

"Even war is mere politics," Nolan said. "The Lady Alyc here—she can confirm what I have told you."

Tedric turned to his left in time to see Alyc fasten Nolan with an ugly glare. She had asked to join them on this mission, promising to be good. This was the first time she had accompanied them to a meeting, and Tedric only hoped her promise meant that she would not choose to betray them now.

She spoke slowly and cautiously, sticking close to the true facts. "My brother is not the proper emperor. Randow, so far as I know, is not dead. Even if he were, one of his cousins should assume the throne."

"See?" said Nolan, attempting to show triumph. "Even his sister says that he's a traitor."

"I said nothing . . ." Alyc began, but she broke off when Nolan glared at her. She sighed, folding her hands. Despite her blindness, Alyc often seemed to sense things that others had to actually see.

The Darkal did not appear to have noticed Alyc's abortive interruption. He said, "But we do not know this man Randow, either. Both are strangers to us and thus our loyalty must lie with the crown and title rather than any man. Nine hundred common-years have passed since the great Emperor Terran visited Narabia and spoke directly to our forefathers. We have seen few men of Earth in that time and no emperors."

"But Randow is the grandchild of Terran, not Matthew."

The Darkal continued to shake his head, unimpressed. "It does not matter."

If it had been Tedric's decision to make, he would have given up here and stolen away into the warm, windy night, but Nolan was more determined. He reached into a pocket of his tunic and drew out a creased sheet of paper. "All we ask is that you add your name to our proclamation of independence. We have visited other tribes before yours and obtained much support."

The Darkal took the proclamation from Nolan and read it carefully. He seemed unimpressed. Tedric wondered if the Darkal might know more than he indicated about their past support. Nolan had exaggerated, if not lied. Most of the tribes they had visited on Narabia had refused them outright. A few, it was true, had agreed, perhaps through politeness, to withhold final judgment until later.

The Darkal handed the paper back to Nolan, then glanced at the silent, impassive faces of the men around him. They seemed to be exchanging secret signals, but it was impossible to guess what these might mean. "We cannot agree to assist you at this

time. Your proclamation states that we refuse to recognize the existence of imperial authority on our
world, and that is not true."

"But there is no other way to defeat Carey," said
Nolan.

"Then we cannot help you. Look," said the Darkal, in a sudden descent from his past formality, "let
us be frank with one another. Should we sign this
proclamation, then what would happen? An imperial
ship filled with armed Corpsmen would visit our
world. There would be fighting, death, disruption of
the sacred travel routes. We cannot permit this."

"You are not cowards," said Nolan.

The Darkal nodded. "But we are not fools."

Even Nolan had to give up then. He tucked the
proclamation away, unsigned as always, and rose to
his feet. He bowed and extended a hand.

The Darkal stood, bowed, and shook. He spoke
quickly, apparently in haste to be done now that the
matter was finished. "We thank you for sharing our
fire. You are welcome to remain among us as you
wish."

"We will go with the dawn," siad Nolan.

"Then we wish you well upon your travels." The
Darkal went out. Ceremoniously, in careful single file,
the old men followed. The wind swept into the tent,
scattering sand.

Alone, Nolan glared at Tedric and Wilson. "It's
hopeless, you know that," he said. "They've got to be

in contact with one another. The refusals are too coincidental; the arguments they use are always the same. I don't care how primitive these people look, they've got radios hidden away somewhere."

"Does it matter?" said Tedric.

"It matters when I tell a little lie and they know it's a lie."

"Then tell the truth," Lady Alyc suggested from the floor.

Nolan frowned at her, but there was nothing he could say.

"I think it's time we gave up on this world," Wilson said. He was the one who had suggested visiting Narabia in the first place. He had heard of the natives' reputation as keen fighters. "Even if we do get a Darkal or two to sign our proclamation, what's it going to mean? There's a thousand tribes on the planet and we're not going to visit them all."

"Yes, we can go," Nolan agreed, "but then what? Where next? Gopal again, or Lindamar?" These were planets where they had been refused before. "The trouble with these backworlders is that they're not as stupid as they look. They already know we're outlaws with nothing much to lose. They know we've got one little ship, the *Vishnu*, and they know that's not enough to bring down an empire that's stood for centuries."

"Why not tell them more lies?" said Alyc. "Tell them you've got a thousand ships."

"Because they're smart enough to see," Nolan said. "We haven't been lucky enough to hit upon a planet of blind men."

"Wouldn't do you any good," Alyc said firmly. "They can smell, and your lies stink."

"You'd think so. He's your brother."

"I loathe my brother," she said, so sharply that no one could doubt it was true.

"But you think we ought to quit and crawl home."

"On the contrary," said Alyc. "What I think is that you're all three acting like a bunch of unimaginative, gutless cowards. You're trying to fool people, not help them."

"Care to take over?" said Nolan, with an attempt at mockery.

"Care to let me?" said Alyc. She laughed in a high, lilting singsong voice and swept gracefully to her feet. "Now, gentlemen and robot, if you don't greatly mind, I am bored and I am tired. You can stay here and listen to the wind and your own arguments all night, but I'd like to get some rest. Tedric," she held out a thin, bronzed hand, "would you see me to my chopper, please."

"Yes, of course, Alyc. I'll take you."

"No, you'll guide me," she said. "I'll take myself."

"I'm sorry. I didn't mean to imply—"

She laughed, touching his arm. "Tedric, I don't care what you meant. Whatever it was, you're forgiven. Now, please, let's go."

He was never quite sure of her reaction—or her

meaning. What were her feelings now? Wilson had sent Melor Carey a number of demands for ransom, but so far, no reply of any kind had been received. This silence surprised Tedric, but Alyc seemed quite undisturbed. Why?

They went outside. The brutal wind seemed somehow less fierce here than it had in the tent. Tedric placed a hand across his forehead to shield his eyes from the driven sand. Alyc, of course, needed no such protection. In the sky, a trio of tiny white moons glowed and glittered. The wind wiped the night sky free of clouds and showed the shining stars in their full splendor. The chopper lay forty meters from the edge of the nomad encampment.

Talk was nearly impossible over the howling wind, and Tedric had intended to remain silent until they reached the chopper. Alyc, too, on occasions like this, when she was alone with one or another of her captors, seemed to prefer saying nothing. This time, she surprised Tedric. Even though she almost had to shout to be heard, she said, "I'm glad you came with me, Tedric."

He shouted, too, though politely. "I don't mind. Wilson and Phillip will talk and talk. There's really nothing to say."

"There's something I've been meaning to ask."

His surprise increased. What could she possibly have to ask him? "Oh?"

"Your name. It's such an odd one. How did you ever come by it?"

Alyc, of course, knew nothing of his history or

true position. He wasn't deliberatey concealing anything from her, but she had never asked and he saw
no reason to volunteer. To answer her now would
require a lengthy explanation, and with the wind, this
didn't seem the time for something like that. So he
told her, "It's just a name—that's all."

"Just that, though? Just Tedric?"

"I have no family, if that's what you mean."

"No, it's not that. I—" She stopped suddenly and
spun, gripping his arm tightly in both her hands.
There was a new expression on her face, one more
serious than any he had seen before, and he sensed
that she had made a very important decision. "I want
to know if you've ever been called Lord Tedric of the
Marshes."

He couldn't have been more amazed if she'd told
him she knew his natural mother. Lord Tedric of the
Marshes was the name he heard in his own dreams. It
was his old name, his real name, the one he'd had in
that other place where he was born and lived before
the Scientists brought him here. Even Phillip Nolan
did not know Tedric's full and original name. There
was no possible way Alyc could know. "Where have
you heard that name? Did your brother say it, your
father?"

His anxiety must have seemed like anger to her.
Alyc tried to twist away from him. "I . . . please. Tedric, don't hurt me. It wasn't them—it was me."

"What do you mean it was you?" He tried to control his voice, but with the wind, that was impossible.
"I won't harm you. Just tell me."

"It—it's voices in my head. They talk and I listen and sometimes I've heard them say Lord Tedric of the Marshes."

"Who talks? What voices? Where do you hear them? Here? Where?"

She was shaking her head, still struggling in his grasp. "I hear them everywhere, always. Tedric, let me go. I can't talk."

He knew she was right. This was no place. He eased his hold on her and steered her toward the chopper. As he did, she fell against him, as if in exhaustion, and he suddenly realized the great expenditure of energy it had taken for her to confide in him. She wasn't joking about these mysterious voices. He doubted that she had ever been as serious in her life. She had known his name. How?

Carefully, he led her up the steel ladder into the chopper bay. Keller and Ky-shan sat on opposite sides of a table, playing a game with cards.

The *Vishnu* lay hidden in a protected canyon a quarter of the way across the globe. It might have been smarter to have left at least one of them with the ship, but no one had stepped forward to volunteer. Keller looked up when he heard the clatter of Tedric's boots and said, "Any luck with the local bunch?"

"No more than anywhere else," Tedric said. Keller stared at Alyc. Her dishevelment was plain to see. Tedric pretended he didn't notice. "I'm afraid it's hopeless."

Keller nodded, but his eyes still watched Alyc. "I think they might be onto us. I've been playing with the radio and getting funny signals. I think there's someone operating on a sealed channel."

"That's what Wilson thinks, too." Tedric turned Alyc away. "I'm going to take her to her room." A corner of the bay had been partitioned off to provide Alyc some privacy.

"Better watch out," Keller said. "That cat fiend is back there. I asked her if she wanted to share a brew and she went straight for my eyes."

Tedric laughed. "If I can't control her, I'll call for help."

"And I'll send Ky-shan. I'm deaf myself."

Tedric opened the door to Alyc's room and stepped through. Kisha, the subwoman, glowered at him and hissed.

Tedric leaned close to Alyc and whispered. "Are you still willing to talk to me about your voices?"

She nodded. "I am."

"Then we ought to be alone."

"Yes." Alyc stepped forward with sudden bold authority. Here in her own quarters she needed no guiding hand. "Kisha, go stay with the others. I wish to talk to Tedric alone."

"I cannot leave you, Alyc," said Kisha, with firmness. She folded her furry arms and spread her tiny feet.

"You will leave, Kisha."

"Your father would not permit it."

"My father is not here—I am. You are my servant, not his. Kisha, I am commanding you. Please go."

Kisha managed to hold her ground for a few more moments, then her shoulders sagged and her head dipped. "You will be careful, Alyc."

"Of course I will."

"If there is trouble, you will scream."

"Kisha, there's been no trouble so far. Tedric is a gentleman and, even if he were not, what could we do against him?"

"I would tear the eyeballs from his head so that he would never see again," Kisha said, with a flash of old fire.

Alyc laughed. "I'm sure you would, Kisha, but please, for now, do go."

Kisha glared at Tedric a moment longer, then made her departure. Through the thin wall separating them from the central chopper bay, Tedric heard Keller emit a low mournful wail. He laughed. "I hope she doesn't tear their eyeballs out."

"Don't worry. She'll ignore them. For her, that's insult enough."

"Won't you sit down?"

Alyc nodded. "I was just about to." Without help, she maneuvered herself into place in front of the one chair in the room and dropped effortlessly down. "Now what is it that you want to know? You must promise not to shout at me. I've told no one about the voices before."

"Why not?" Tedric endeavored to keep his voice as pleasant as possible. He didn't understand Alyc's tranformed attitude but assumed that would make itself clear in time. Before, she had never treated him with the same open hostility as Wilson and Nolan, but she had hardly been friendly, either.

"Because I believed they would think I was mad."

"And you trust me?"

"Only because . . . because I heard your name. It came again today, as clear as the pounding of a drum. *Lord Tedric of the Marshes.* Of course I had to know. You see, I thought—I hoped—"

"Yes, what?" he said, urging her on.

"I hoped that maybe you heard the voices, too."

He shook his head, negligent as always of the fact that she could not see. "I'm afraid I don't."

"But you alone know that I'm not making it up. I know your name, Tedric, and I can tell that no one else does."

It was always possible, of course, that she might be lying. Melor Carey, even Matthew, might somehow have discovered his true identity and told her of it. But he didn't think so. He believed her. "Then tell me more about these voices. How do you hear them? Where? When? Do you have any idea who they are?"

"None. I never . . . I used to wonder, but there seemed no point. They come to me whenever I want to listen. There are two of them, actually—two sets. One is very different from the other, but I can hear them both."

"There's more than one person involved—more than one voice."

"There are many. Some I almost know. Not by name. They never use names. By tone."

"Then these are actual voices? You hear the words?"

She shook her head. "Not words, no. Thoughts. And just sometimes for that, too. It's more like music than talking—thought music."

"And you hear these voices now?"

"If I wished, I could. I've heard them nearly all my life, almost as far back as I can remember. At first I was frightened. Some of the voices are terrible— ugly, foul. Most are beautiful. When I was growing up, I came to depend on them. They were my only friends. But I grew afraid. I thought I was crazy be- cause they went on and on and nobody else ever heard anything. That's why I went on the *Oceania* into space. I thought if I was away from Milrod Eleven, they would not follow. But they did."

"As strong as before?"

"Stronger, or the same. It's hard to say."

Tedric tried to fit what she was telling him with what he already knew of her life. One thing disturbed him, the one thing that set Alyc apart from other women. "You said you'd always heard the voices. Tell me this. Before your accident—before you lost your sight—did you hear them then?"

"I have always—" But her mouth slammed sud- denly shut. She tensed in her chair and almost seemed to tremble. "I didn't."

"You're sure about that? You're positive?"

"I . . . I . . . yes. I never thought about it before. I guess I didn't want to. I hate the accident. I hate thinking about it, remembering how it happened, the pain. But it's true. When I was recovering, when I couldn't stand or move around, when the medical technicians were still trying to give me new eyes, that's when I first heard them."

Tedric nodded unconsciously. He couldn't help her. What she'd told him was a raw fact; evaluation would have to come later. "Alyc, will you do one thing for me?"

"Yes, what?"

"Listen to your voices. See if you can do it right now with me in the room. Listen and then tell me—at the same time, if it's possible—exactly what you're hearing."

"I don't know if I can."

"Then tell me afterward. You'll try, won't you?"

She nodded at last. "I'll try."

"Thank you." He was reserving final judgment. He knew she wasn't lying deliberately and knew, from the evidence of his name, that there was more to this than simple delusion. But what? Having her talk was the only means he could discover for answering that.

Her lips were pressed tightly together. Her jaw was firm. She was not a beautiful woman, he decided, although at first he had thought that she was. Not beautiful, but not pretty, either. No one word could truly encompass what Alyc Carey was. A narrow, skrunken face, the skin drawn smoothly across big bones. A high bald forehead. Thick black hair pulled straight up in a wild, frizzy fluff. And the empty eyes.

That was what made any description so difficult. When he looked at Alyc, Tedric always saw those unseeing sockets; they dominated everything that surrounded them.

She said, distantly, "I can hear them Tedric."

"What are they saying?"

"Blackness." She could have been asleep, or in a trance. Her voice lacked energy, a dead tone.

"That's what you hear?"

"It's what I feel, yes."

"Who is speaking?" He remembered what she had said about hearing two sets of voices. It might be important. "Can you tell?"

"It is warm."

"Nice?"

"Gentle. Warm, gentle, soothing."

"But they talk of blackness."

"Of black forces, dark things. An enemy. I see a monster with black fur and a painted face. It is huge but unreal. It is part of the blackness."

"Does this monster have a name?"

"There are no names."

"Only mine?"

"No names."

He wondered if she knew who he was anymore. He no longer doubted the truth of her words. She was definitely hearing something. Voices. "Is there anything more you can tell, Alyc? Anything more you can hear?"

"I hear the numbers. They talk always in numbers. Numbers and symbols, rarely words. I do not understand the numbers."

"But is there anything you do understand?"

"The blackness and . . . " She hesitated, like a person groping to fix a distant sight.

"Yes?" he proded.

"And the red things. Alive. Spreading, always spreading. The red things that are the black things. They speak often of them."

Tedric felt a chill of recognition. What Alyc was describing sounded frighteningly similar to the red clouds that had invaded the Wykzl nation. Only a handful of men knew anything at all about these clouds. Melor Carey was one of them. Could that explain it? "Anything more?"

"Lord Tedric of the Marshes."

"They speak of me?"

"Tedric and the danger. His danger. A chill. Cold." She began to shiver. Her teeth chattered. Her body shook. Her bare skin grew bumps. "The chill is fear."

He was concerned and considered forcing her to awake. But she had spoken of personal danger. He must know. "What is this danger that Tedric faces?"

"I can't . . . "

"You can't say?"

"They don't say. It is known to all of them, and they are afraid. They don't talk."

Her shivering had grown less intense. He decided not to disturb her, to try to find out more. "Can you tell me if there's any connection between—"

He stopped. She was staring at him. Not with her eyes—no, of course not—but with her thoughts. She was awake.

"They've stopped talking," she said.

"You're awake?"

"They've stopped talking to watch. It's happened before. Something important is about to happen somewhere, and they want to observe."

He came toward her. She seemed no worse for the ordeal she had endured. He took her hands in his and drew her to her feet. "Why don't we go and get something to eat?"

"I . . . " She smiled with sudden gratitude. "I am hungry, but—you didn't tell me what I said."

"Don't you know?"

She shook her head. "I did talk to you? All I remember is what I heard. I don't remember what I said."

"Do you remember hearing about me?"

"Your name? I remember that, vaguely, but I—"

Then it hit.

The first bomb went off with the impact of a huge fist slamming into the ground. The floor rose up and the ceiling seemed to come down and Tedric reached out and grabbed Alyc to protect her. He felt the warmth of her body through the thin tunic she wore. They hit the floor locked in an embrace. Tedric felt his elbow stinging. The rest of him seemed all right.

There was a second explosion, farther off than the first, then a third. He held Alyc tightly in his arms.

Keller burst through the door. "Sir, that's it!" he cried. "That's what it was! The fleet's here. Someone called them. They're dropping bombs on us right now."

"Get to the controls and start the chopper." Tedric sprang to his feet. "Have Wilson and Nolan made it back yet?"

"No, sir, but I'm sure they're on their way—if they can. The first bomb hit the settlement square on. The tents are burning. I know people are dead."

Because of us, Tedric thought. Because we thought we could play a revolutionary game and get away with it. "We'll wait for them as long as we can," he said aloud. "Now move—we can't wait."

As Keller rushed out the door, Kisha rushed in past him. She went to Lady Alyc, who still lay prone on the floor, and cradled her in her furry arms. Alyc glanced up at Tedric and winked. She was all right. He decided to leave her and hurry to help Keller and Ky-shan with the controls. "Don't let her off the floor," he called to Kisha past his shoulder. "Both of you lay flat. With any luck, we'll be out of here in—"

A fourth bomb landed just as he reached the doorway. Another close one. He spread his feet to keep from toppling and struggled to roll with the shock.

In the forward bay, Keller and Ky-shan leaned

over the controls. Tedric could hear the whirring of the rotating chopper blades. "All set and ready to fly," said Keller.

Just then, the outer door fell open and Nolan and Wilson sprawled inside. "What's going on?" Nolan cried. "Who's trying to kill us? It's not the navy, is it?"

Ky-shan was closest to the radio. He turned and said, coolly, "It is the navy. An imperial squadron. They are sending a message now."

Wilson shut the outer door. Keller fingered the controls in a final practice run. Nolan said, "What is the message?"

"They demand your immediate surrender. If you refuse, you will be killed. They call you the space pirates of Quicksilver."

"Damn," said Nolan. "They know everything."

"Should I send a return transmission?" asked Ky-shan.

"Yes," said Wilson. "Call back and tell them to hurry up and go to hell."

As Ky-shan moved to obey, Wilson assumed a place directly behind Keller. "Get this thing off the ground," he commanded.

Just then, another bomb went off. This one was too far away to cause any damage.

But the next one? Tedric wondered.

7 THE DESTRUCTION OF VISHNU

Flight from the Narabian encampment proved no problem for the space pirates of Quicksilver. It was easy—too easy—and that was worse than being difficult.

Almost as soon as Wilson and Nolan arrived, Keller lifted the prop-chopper into the night air. Cruising above the burning encampment, they saw what seened like a vision of hell contained. Here was a fire. There was another. Forty, perhaps as many as fifty, separate conflagrations. The bombs had done their work well. Tedric knew there must be dozens of dead and dying people beneath him. He further knew, even for the living, their lives would never be the same again. Tedric had caused this destruction. He had brought sudden, horrible death to innocent people. He and the pirates. He and their revolution.

It was a measure of guilt he wished he did not have to bear.

Keller did not linger long above the burning tents. He set off immediately southward, flying a zig-zag route that kept the chopper snuggled close to the raw Narabian landscape where any sensory peepers from above would have trouble finding it. Flying this way, using diversionary tactics, it took all of that night plus another day and night to reach the secluded can-yon where the *Vishnu* lay hidden. As Keller cautiously sought a safe resting place for the chopper among the rocky terrain, Wilson stood beside him, arms folded, a frown on his face. "Anything yet?" he asked Ky-shan, who continued to monitor the radio.

"Not a word," said the Wykzl. "I've found the channel they used before, but now it's silent, too. Ei-ther they're not broadcasting or they've switched channels again."

"Probably the latter," said Wilson. "Well, keep trying. There's got to be something."

"All right."

Since the original call for surrender, they had not heard a peep from the imperial navy.

Nolan tried to act triumphant. "We've beaten their tails," he told Wilson, "and they're too embar-rassed to acknowledge it. We called their bluff with strong words. I wouldn't be surprised if they're al-ready on their way home."

Wilson, whose sense of humor did not extend quite as far as Nolan's, shook his head. "Even you know better than that, Nolan."

"Of course I know better. It's just that I don't care to know that I know, if you get what I mean."

The *Vishnu*, when they reached her, seemed no worse for their absence. They went aboard the ship, and Wilson decided to abandon the chopper where it had landed. "I don't think we'll need it where we're going," he said.

"And where's that?" said Nolan, who continued to feign a cocky air.

"You'll find out soon enough."

Aboard the *Vishnu*, Wilson called everyone together in the control room. It had been obvious to Tedric for some time that Wilson had a fair idea why the navy had so suddenly lost interest in its apparent prey. From the scattered pattern of the bombing, Tedric himself guessed there had been no more than a single shuttle above them. Ky-shan's description of a naval squadron had not been entirely true. Wilson leaned close to the instrument panel, making tiny adjustments in a set of controls. The sensory apparatus, Tedric guessed. Wilson wanted to get a clear reading on what might lurk above.

When at last Wilson turned away from the controls, his gloomy face betrayed the nature of his discoveries. It never ceased to amaze Tedric that a robot like Wilson, a heartless creature of wire and steel, wore his deepest feelings so close to the surface. "All right, we'd better talk," Wilson said. "I'll tell you what I know."

"What you know or what you don't know?" asked Lady Alyc. She had specifically asked to be included in the meeting, and Wilson had agreed. Kisha was present, too, unusually quiet.

"Both," said Wilson. He raised two fingers. "For a start, this is the number of choices we have left."

"It does beat this," Nolan said, raising one finger.

"But not by much," Wilson said.

"Then tell us what the choices are and let us decide," Alyc said.

Wilson frowned. "I intend to. For a start, there's only one ship in orbit above us, but if I read the sensors right, it's a cruiser and a damned big one, the biggest I've seen anywhere."

"The *Eagleseye*," Nolan guessed, referring to the ship on which he and Tedric had served with Matthew Carey.

"More than likely," Wilson agreed. "Which means, if the navy sent its strongest ship here, they're pretty damned sure who they're after and why. I'd also guess, for various reasons, that, though they knew we were on Narabia, they weren't sure exactly where. I think they sent a number of shuttles down. They hit a bunch of encampments, hoping when they got around to us that we'd expose ourselves. That's what happened. We didn't have any choice and we ran."

"But if that's the case," Tedric said, "it doesn't explain why they didn't at least try to follow us here. The *Eagleseye* is the most sophisticated ship in the imperial arsenal. Its sensory network should have been able to follow our course no matter how much we zigged and zagged and hugged the landscape."

"Maybe the *Eagleseye* was on the other side of the planet when they struck."

"That's possible, yes," Tedric said, "but it's also bad planning. Wilson said the navy must have known all along we were on Narabia. That's the part I really don't follow. What good did it do them to scare us out, if they already knew we were here and didn't intend following us?"

"My guess is that they were less interested in adding to their own store of information," Wilson said, "and more interested in adding to ours. They knew we were here. They wanted us to know they were there. You see, the *Vishnu's* got to be a bit of a problem for them. It looks like an ordinary battletug but it moves at N-space velocities. They can't possibly know how keen our sensory network happens to be. My guess is that they were hoping we couldn't spot the *Eagleseye* in orbit. They wanted to scare us into making a run off the planet."

"But what would they do then?" Nolan said. "Try to follow us home to Quicksilver?"

"I doubt that they ever intended to let us get that far."

"I don't understand," Nolan said.

"I think I do," said Tedric. He was a keen student of the tactics of space warfare. "Narabia possesses a magnetic field, I believe."

Wilson nodded. "It does indeed."

Then Tedric knew for certain he was on the right path. He told the others, "It's a tactic that the Wykzl often used during the war to establish a planetwide blockade. One cruiser in orbit launches a heatray straight into the field. It becomes a part of that field. Then any object, including an enemy spacecraft, that unknowingly penetrates the field is burned to a crisp."

"It's like a steel door," Wilson confirmed. "A steel door slammed in our faces."

"But at least we know about it," Nolan said.

"Which does us no good at all," Wilson siad. "The *Vishnu,* of course, has no screens. Whether we know it or not, if we try to leave Narabia, we'll still be burned to death."

"I thought you said something about two choices," Alyc said.

"I did. And that's one of them. We can stay here, hunker down, and hope that eventually the *Eagleseye* steams away and leaves us free to depart."

"Then that's what we'll do," said Nolan.

Tedric shook his head. "I don't think they'll be willing to wait. They've already indicated what they're capable of doing in the interests of justice. They didn't hesitate a moment before burning that settlement. It probably wasn't the only one. They won't hesitate the next time, either."

Wilson nodded solemnly. "That's my guess, too. They'll enlist the natives—blackmail them with examples of slaughter if necessary—to help spot us. Even here, where it looks so desolate, they'll find us in time."

"Then what's your other choice?" Nolan said.

"The obvious one. We try to make a run for it."

"But I thought you said that was suicide."

"Normally, it would be, but again, the *Vishnu* is different. The magnetic field tactic was developed for use against interplanetary shuttles. The *Vishnu* can travel through normal space at a velocity fifty times that of a shuttle. We just might make it. Think of a hand passing through a flame. If you do it quick enough, you get singed. If you leave it there, you burn."

"And you think the *Vishnu* can move that quickly?"

Wilson shook his head. "I think the chances are damned remote."

"Then maybe we ought to stay," Nolan said. "Better an uncertain death than a certain one."

"They both sound equally certain to me," Alyc put in. "I'd prefer the quick to the slow."

"Shall we take a vote?" said Nolan.

"I think we should," said Wilson.

"Then I vote to stay," Nolan said.

"Go," said Alyc.

"Stay," said Keller.

"Go," said Tedric.

"Go," said Wilson.

"I must vote with Alyc," said Kisha.

"You don't have to if you don't want to," Alyc told her.

"No, I do," Kisha said.

"And you, Ky-shan?" said Wilson, turning to the Wykzl. "You're one of us, too."

The alien hesitated at first, plainly surprised that he had even been asked. Tedric thought Ky-shan most likely would not choose to vote, but the Wykzl surprised him. "I elect to go," Ky-shan said, "because there is a tale told among my people of a great warrior hero who, because of the blessed speed of his ship, broke the barrier of heat. I believe if one can succeed, so can another. We must try."

"See? Then it can be done," said Nolan, who appeared to have forgotten his own original vote.

"Then the matter's settled," Wilson said. "We go."

Tedric crossed the room to where Alyc stood and suggested that she and Kisha remain in their room while the *Vishnu* made its run. She smiled patiently, but shook her head. "If I'm going to die, I'd prefer to watch it happening, not be caught by surprise."

"It may not be very pleasant out here," he said.

"And your father will not like it," said Kisha.

"Then why doesn't he do something about it?" she said.

"Alyc, that's hardly fair," Kisha said.

"It's his navy, isn't it? They didn't come this far without orders."

This was a factor Tedric had not considered until

now. But, yes, of course, he thought. Ever since he and Alyc had spoken about her voices, he had almost ceased to regard her as what she no doubt still was: their prisoner—a hostage. Did the *Eagleseye* commander above have any idea that Lady Alyc Carey was a passenger aboard the ship he intended to destroy? And, if he was made aware of that fact, what would his reaction then be? Would he dare proceed with his original plan? Tedric considered the obvious possibilities. He could contact the *Eagleseye*, speak to the commander. Threaten, cajole, demand. Use Alyc Carey as a means for saving all their lives. Such an attempt would, of course, be riddled with traps. A radio message might well risk exposing their present position. The commander might simply refuse to go contrary to his established orders. But wasn't it worth it? Couldn't it be tried?

Tedric looked at Alyc and realized that, no, it could not be tried. He would never consent to using her as a bargaining tool. To do that would necessitate, at some point in the negotiations, agreeing to return her to her father's care. He would never do that. This was not another of his feelings. It had nothing to do with the still unresolved mystery of her secret voices. He did not want to use Alyc. He wanted to free her from being used and, if she returned to her father, that could never possibly happen. None of this was anything he had consciously considered before. He knew it was a direct result of his talk with her in the private room of the chopper, and he knew it had a lot to do with pity and sympathy. He didn't want her to die, but he didn't want her to return to a living death, either. Perhaps the decision was not properly his to make. Perhaps he was taking too many godly powers into his own hands. Not only Alyc's life but his own and those of the other pirates lay in the balance. But he decided. Again, it wasn't a definite feeling. He just knew what was right, and he did it.

"All right, then stay," he told her at last, "but do try to keep back out of the way. When we take off, it's going to have to be all at once—*whoosh*. There won't be time for bumping into each other."

"I'll be as inconspicuous as a little ghost," she said.

And Tedric believed that Alyc, if she wished, could even be that.

Wilson raised his right hand high over his head and tolled off the final few seconds. In the rear of the ship, the big N-space drive roared and howled. The floor beneath vibrated from the suppressed fury erupting behind. Wilson said, "Ten . . . nine . . . eight . . . seven . . ."

Tedric handled the ship's controls, a relatively simple task. Whatever route they used to leave Narabia, the planet's magnetic field would be waiting to greet them. The best course to follow was therefore the most direct. Attaining escape velocity presented no problem. In order to survive, the *Vishnu* would have to exceed that speed by at least ten times. The

Eagleseye presently lay out of sight in orbit above the opposite hemisphere of Narabia. Tedric found a certain satisfaction in that fact. It meant, if the *Vishnu* did burn to a crisp, that no one would be near enough to observe. A man's death ought to be a private act, he believed. Having died previously in his life, Tedric knew this as well as anyone.

"Six . . . five . . . four . . . " said Wilson.

Ky-shan leaned close to the radio. The *Eagleseye* had still made no effort to contact them, and Tedric was secretly glad of that. A request for surrender coming at this time might have seemed too tempting to resist. Alyc and Kisha huddled in an inconspicuous corner of the room. Keller stood behind Ky-shan and chewed his long fingernails. Nolan, in a chair, kept his eyes shut. There was perspiration on his forehead. But he was also smiling. It was a crazy grin—without pleasure— but a grin.

"Three . . . two . . . one . . . " said Wilson.

Tedric leaned foward and touched the acceleration lever. There was silence all around. Everyone held his breath. Me, too, Tedric thought. The air in his lungs seemed sweeter than usual. It might well be the last he ever tasted.

"Zero," said Wilson.

Tedric jerked the acceleration lever.

With a heaving shudder, the *Vishnu* immediately responded. Like a bullet driven from the barrel of a gun—only much faster—the ship exploded away from the Narabian surface.

Tedric tried to follow what happened in the viewscreen above his head, but everything seemed to move so quickly. There was a flash of color—blue— the sky—then dancing yellow flecks—the stars. It happened all in an instant. He had no time in which to analyze what he was seeing.

The heat came almost at once. He had expected something gradual, but this was like being hit by a wave of lightning. The heat burst inside him and seemed to spread outward toward his skin. His lungs burned. His breath was like a flame. He couldn't see, think, or even cry out. The pain was overwhelming. Everything around him burned bright red. He couldn't bear to sit, but when he sprang to his feet, the heat from the floor burned through his boots and seared the soles of his feet.

"We aren't making it," Wilson said calmly. As a robot, Wilson was not affected by the pain. "We're going to burn up."

Tedric hurled a wild fist at the control panel. He hit the ship's automatic lock, wanting to ensure that, even in death, the *Vishnu* would continue its hurtling assault into open space. He didn't want to be found. He didn't want the cold, unfeeling eyes of some anonymous sailor staring at his own burned carcass. Space was the eternal graveyard. It was a fitting place for him to lie.

But his eyes caught the viewscreen, and he stopped. For a moment, the pain and the fire were forgotten. He leaned forward, squinting through misty eyes. There was something to be seen. A creature. A huge, misshapen metal thing. A monster. It came straight toward the *Vishnu's* bow, and it's cavernous mouth hung open, like a feeding fish.

We are dead and about to be eaten, Tedric thought.

But the thought made no sense. Neither did the thing in the viewscreen. Delusion. Hallucination. A madman's crazed fantasy.

But then he realized that the metal monster was not a living creature at all: it was a ship.

But that was impossible, too. There was only one ship here, the *Eagleseye*, and it was presently far away. Besides, this ship didn't resemble an imperial cruiser in the least respect; the *Eagleseye* had no yawning mouth.

He could think no more. His feet, his lungs, his lips, his tongue, his eyes, his skin—he was burning up. Dimly, he could see the others wrestling with the pain. Only Wilson was untouched—and Alyc. She sat as she had sat in the beginning. Her mouth was tense. Her jaw was firm. Her face showed the pain she must be feeling, but there was no other outright sign. She didn't cry. She didn't squirm. She sat bolt upright.

Tedric stumbled toward her and reached out. She was like a cool oasis.

He tripped.

Fell.

There was blackness.

And the infernal heat.

8 MO-LEETE MAKES AN OFFER

In a dream, Tedric saw Ky-shan the Wykzl floating above him in the air, a disembodied head. The dream was like a cool embrace. He remembered another time when he was burning, and this was much better. Still, there was that floating alien head, and that was not right. Its tendrils twitched. Its lips moved. There was a sound, not a voice.

Then he realized he wasn't dreaming.

For a moment, he thought he was dead, but that was wrong, too.

He was awake and alive.

He was gloriously cool.

And the face that loomed above him: he recognized it now. It wasn't Ky-shan.

"Mo-leete," he said aloud. The sound was strange in his own ears. The voice did not seem to belong to him.

But the face smiled. "Then you do remember me, friend Tedric?"

"But where—where am I?" He knew how silly

that must sound, but what other question should he ask? "I am alive, aren't I?"

"As far as we can tell, you are." A second hovering head loomed into place beside Mo-leete. Tedric recognized this one, too. It was Wilson, the renegade robot, commander-in-chief of the infamous space pirates of Quicksilver. Wilson also smiled.

Tedric sat bolt upright. He, Wilson, and Mo-leete were alone in an oblong-shaped room. The walls were formed from a dull burnished metal that Tedric could not immediately identify and, except for the cot on which he sat, there were no furnishings of any kind. A matching pair of broad round doors stood closed at each end of the room.

"Where am I?" he said again, voicing the question that was most important to him.

Wilson answered. He and Mo-leete had grown bodies now, and they seemed less alien and threatening than before. "In space. N-space. This is Mo-leete's ship, and he's saved our lives."

Tedric rubbed his head. The temples kept throbbing, in and out, in and out, a rhythmic booming. "When I first saw you, I thought I was dreaming. I thought—are you sure I'm not dead?" He gripped his skull tightly.

"If you are," Wilson said softly, "then I must apologize for being here. I know I'm not dead."

"Nor am I," said Mo-leete.

"I remember the ship," Tedric said. "The *Vishnu*. We tried to break the heat barrier and failed. I remember the heat, the pain."

"Is that all you remember?" asked Wilson.

Tedric nodded slowly, but that answer wasn't exactly true.

"No, there was something else. At the end, in the viewscreen, I saw something I thought was a metal monster with a gaping mouth. Then I realized it was a ship."

"That was my cruiser," Mo-leete said. "I had the hatch open to catch you. It worked, too. Another few seconds, and there'd have been nothing left to save."

"You saved all of us?"

"He did," said Wilson.

"Then where are they? The others . . . Alyc?"

"Still being tended by medical robots," Mo-leete said. "If all goes right, they should be with us shortly. I understood your condition was somewhat better than the others, so I had you brought here. Perhaps I was wrong." He pressed gently on Tedric's chest, forcing him back down against the cot. "You should rest."

"But you shouldn't even be here," Tedric said. He thought a portion of his disorientation originated in the strange geometry of this room. It was like nothing he had ever seen before, not simply unfamiliar, but alien. It was a room in a Wykzl spacecraft and should not be expected to look like home. "You have intruded upon the territory of the Empire."

"That could be a point of debate," Mo-leete said, musingly. "We are in N-space at the present, and how can something which, physically, is nothing be said to belong to one race of creatures?"

"Narabia wasn't in N-space."

"I was lost when I strayed there."

Tedric grinned. "You're a liar, Mo-leete."

"And not a very capable one, I'm afraid."

"But a kind one. You did save my life."

"Didn't I once vow that I would? Remember, Tedric, I gave you my oath as part of the ritual of surrender. I promised to protect you forevermore. For me to let you burn to death without lifting a hand would have been an act of terrible cowardice and disgrace."

"Whatever your reasons, I thank you." Tedric shook his head weakly. He had heard of last second rescues before, but this one approached the brink of unbelievability. Coincidence could justify some of the things that had occurred but not everything. He knew Mo-leete had more to explain than what he had so far revealed. But his head ached. Further revelations would have to wait for an easing of this private pain.

The door at the farthest end of the room suddenly dilated. Tedric turned and saw a robot. Then another. And another. These were Wykzl robots, true metal monsters without the human form of Wilson. Each robot led another creature by the arm. Keller came first, then Nolan. There was Ky-shan and Kisha. Alyc was the last to enter the room.

"Alyc!" cried Tedric, attempting to spring to his feet.

But Mo-leete held him fast. "No, be calm, friend Tedric. These people are as ill as you. We must move slowly."

With Mo-leete holding him, Tedric could not move at all. The procession of robots swept into the room and formed a circle around his cot. Suddenly, from underneath the floor, a set of padded chairs materialized. Each robot placed its burden upon one of the chairs. While Mo-leete restrained Tedric, Wilson went over and spoke to each of the pirates in turn. He spoke softly, and Tedric could not hear a word.

Alyc was the last one Wilson consulted. At last, spinning away from her, Wilson held up his hands and grinned. "It's safe," he said. "Let Tedric go. Everyone's convinced he's going to live."

And they did.

On the second day subsequent to the pirates' first awakening, Mo-leete at last consented to Tedric's repeated requests that he explain what was going on. Mo-leete agreed to hold a meeting, during which he would tell what he could and answer what he should. "We are approaching our destination, so perhaps it is best that you have some inkling of the facts before we arrive," said Mo-leete.

Until this moment, Tedric had been unaware that they possessed a particular destination. "Where are we going?" he asked.

Mo-leete winked broadly. "If I told you that, what would be the point of holding a meeting to explain?"

Tedric could not very well answer that, and Mo-leete seemed pleased by his failure.

The meeting was convened in the ship's central control room. The sight of so much wondrous technology made Tedric sick with envy. Under any circumstances except the most extraordinary, Mo-leete's ship functioned automatically. A central computer no bigger than one wall of the control room handled every conceivable ship's function, including navigation, course correction, and N-space proximity. Mo-leete was the only crew member aboard, but even he appeared to have nothing specific to do. The robots functioned only in a service capacity. The control room clicked, buzzed, clacked and whirred. Mo-leete, as he called the meeting to order, seemed unconcerned and oblivious to the activity surrounding him.

All of the pirates were present, including Alyc and Kisha. Wilson had opposed letting Alyc attend. "Whatever brought Mo-leete all this way," he said, "has got to be pretty important. I know you've grown to like her, though I can't for the life of me figure out how, but she is still the daughter of our prime enemy, and we can't trust her too far. Admittedly she's done nothing to harm us so far, but I don't think it's wise to lay too much temptation in her path."

Tedric was stubbornly convinced of exactly the opposite. He believed the more temptation for Alyc, the better, because it was only through temptation that she would learn who her true friends were. Tedric had long since decided that Alyc would never return home—though he had never revealed this decision to anyone, including Alyc—and he felt it was important to prove to her that she was trusted.

Wilson finally gave in. The only reason he did was because, at the scheduled time of the meeting, Alyc and Kisha both appeared in the control room, and nobody was inclined to try to force them to leave.

Mo-leete did not seem to care, either. He took a place in the center of the others, like a teacher preparing to lecture an attentive classroom, and said, "My recent rescue of you and your ship was not sheer coincidence."

For Tedric, this came as no surprise. He leaned forward in his chair, straining to hear past the clicking of the room, and waited to be further illuminated.

Mo-leete said, "Because, you see, at the time the incident occurred, I was actively seeking you out. I would, in fact, have reached Narabia slightly before the imperial cruiser, but when I discovered its near approach, I decided to wait and see what would develop."

"My poor burned body thanks you for that," Phillip Nolan said.

Mo-leete smiled. Like most of his race, he had long ago learned the etiquette of human gesture and tended to make use of this knowledge more than was really necessary. "I do apologize for the suffering you endured, friend Phillip, but I preferred not to expose my existence to the imperial cruiser if it could be avoided. Fortunately, I was able to save you and stay hidden at the same time, and I think that was best for all of us. Now, to return to my original purpose, I have an offer to make you."

Tedric nodded. He had expected something like

this, but really had no idea what might follow. Wilson, a look of concern on his face, glanced at Tedric, then at Alyc. She, with Kisha protectively at her side, leaned anxiously forward in her chair. She was listening to Mo-leete with interest, oblivious to everything else.

Mo-leet went on. "From our own sphere, my brothers have overhead radio descriptions of your recent exploits, and some interest was aroused. When it became increasingly clear that you were no longer following a crass pattern of common, space piracy, I was called in to state an opinion. Our sensors had determined your identities, and I stated what I knew of your respective pasts. A decision was eventually reached that you were conscious revolutionaries, and I was ordered to undertake a mission of direct contact. Put bluntly, the Wykzl nation sympathizes with your cause. We further realize the immense, if not to say insurmountable, difficulties you face in bringing this cause to actual fruition. For that reason, I have come to offer help."

Tedric frowned. He did not like the sound of Mo-leete's offer. Whatever the nature of his personal relationship with specific individuals like Mo-leete and Ky-shan, Tedric well knew that the Wykzl, as a nation, remained mankind's oldest enemy. Accepting help from them smacked loudly of treason. This was definitely something he would have to hear more about to decide. "What sort of help do you have in mind, Mo-leete?" The suspiciousness in his voice showed clearly.

"Crucial help," Mo-leete said. "We are not fools. The one thing blocking success is your lack of strategic material. To overthrow the Careys you need force. With no ships at your disposal, all you can do is talk."

"Talking hasn't done much good." Wilson put in.

Mo-leete nodded, more broadly than was really necessary. "And that is why I have come to offer you ships."

"What kind of ships?" said Tedric.

Mo-leete jerked his head toward the floor. "Our most sophisticated battle cruisers. Exact duplicates of this ship."

Tedric knew what that could mean. A lone man could operate one of these ships. There would be no need to raise a navy to fight a war. "How many ships are you talking about?"

"Only as many as you need," Mo-leete said slowly. "A hundred should do as a start."

Tedric was unable fully to conceal his surprise. He knew the cost of a hundred fully equipped battle cruisers, and the depth of Mo-leete's generosity seemed almost overwhelming. Too overwhelming, Tedric decided. He didn't trust the Wykzl one spare centimeter. "And who would pilot these cruisers?" he asked. "Wykzl sailors?"

Mo-leete shook his head, as though the very concept distressed him. "This is a civil war within the boundaries of the Empire of Man. Obviously, you would have to recruit your own crews."

Tedric didn't think the matter was all that obvious, but he was willing to accept Mo-leete at his word. He might not trust him, but he did believe him. It was what Mo-leete did not say that concerned him, not what he did say openly. "And what about yourself?"

Mo-leete held out his wide arms, showing empty palms. "That is for you to decide. Frankly, it has been some years, and I would enjoy a good fight. Besides, unlike any of you, I am well experienced at space fleet warfare and would eagerly offer my advice and knowledge."

"And if I don't want you?"

"Then I would return home—naturally."

Tedric didn't like being told what was obvious and what was natural. As for the others, most seemed barely able to restrain their enthusiasm. Wilson, for one, was positively glowing with delight. "I think you've got a smart head on your shoulders, Mo-leete," he said. "A damn smart head."

But Tedric knew the final decision was his to make. Wilson had commanded their obedience when they were merely pirates, but the idea of revolution was Tedric's own, and he was their acknowledged leader now. "Before I say anything," Tedric said, "I want you to answer one simple question for me. Why are your people so eager to help us succeed? An Empire free of the domination of the Careys is going to be a stronger Empire. I can't see how that will help the Wykzl at all."

Mo-leete shrugged. "At the present moment,

Tedric, the nature of what helps the Wykzl can concern only one matter." He seemed especially sincere
in saying this, and it took Tedric a moment to comprehend what he meant. Mo-leete was talking about
the red clouds that had invaded the Wykzl nation and
presently threatened to wipe it out.

"In other words," said Tedric, "by helping us, if
we win, you'll expect help in return."

"Our need for Dalkanium remains as dire as
ever. We can expect no help from the Careys. You are
our last hope, Tedric, short of war."

Tedric nodded. Now that he understood the
Wykzl motivation, everything else made sense, too.
The offer of help could be accepted. He opened his
mouth to say so, when Mo-leete suddenly inter-
rupted. One of the instrument panels along the near
wall had begun to flash in a rythmic pattern. "If you
require more convincing," Mo-leete said, "I believe
we have now arrived at our destination."

Tedric turned and looked at the row of viewscreens behind him. During the course of the meeting, the view had severely altered. No longer was he
looking at the gray sameness of N-space. Now the
screens showed a wider and brighter view of black
space and bright stars. "Where are we?" he asked.

"In a portion of the Empire known as the Claros
region." Mo-leete stood as he talked and crossed to
the flashing panel. "You may check the instruments if
you do not believe me. It is a relatively uninhabited
sector composed largely of young white stars."

"I believe you, Mo-leete." Tedric watched the viewscreens. "But I don't understand what we're supposed to find here."

"You will. You—wait, here it comes now." Mo-leete pointed to the viewscreens. "Watch and you will see. Remember what I said. This is a region of the Empire of Man. This is your home."

Tedric watched. At first, there was nothing but the stars and the void, then the object came into view. It was bright, but it wasn't a star. It was nearly transparent, but it wasn't a dust cloud. And it was huge. As the object in the viewscreens grew closer, he could see that it was at least three times as huge as any of the nearest stars.

It was red.

It was growing.

If the Wykzl could be believed, it was alive.

One of the invading red clouds had at last appeared inside the Empire of Man.

Tedric knew what that meant. If this one had come, others would follow. If this one was small now, it would soon be larger.

Mo-leete spoke softly, "As you can see, Tedric, our crisis has now become a most mutual concern."

Tedric nodded. He knew what that cloud could eventually mean: the extinction of the human race.

He shivered and, in spite of himself, said to Mo-leete: "Would you mind very much turning that picture off?"

Mo-leete nodded. He well understood. "I wouldn't mind in the least."

9 EMPEROR MATTHEW I

Melor Carey, once the most powerful individual in the Empire of Man, was heartsick, homesick, and ready to die.

He occupied a sumptuous private bedroom at the heart of the imperial palace in New Melbourne on Earth. For the past nine days, Melor had lain in this room, moving only when the necessities of life required it. Above his head, the gold encrusted ceiling sparkled as the glimmerings of the afternoon sun pierced a nearby glass window and invaded the room. Melor stared at the ceiling without blinking. He seemed to find solace in the simple beauty of the golden light. Solace, perhaps, but not hope. For Melor Carey, the age of hope had ended now, just short of his one hundred thirty-second common-birthday.

He had made one mistake.

He had disobeyed a command of the black beast.

At the time, he had known the risk involved the greatest gamble of his career. Knowing that, he had gone ahead. Before, great risks had meant great success. But before, the beast was on his side.

Not this time. He had disobeyed the beast, and now the beast was destroying him.

He would have chosen suicide, but that was too cowardly. Old Emperor Kane had gone that route. For Melor Carey, the end would come more placidly but no less certainly. He was waiting to die and he would die. There was no further reason to live.

He had told no one. That was not extraordinary, for in the course of his life, there had been few people with whom to share his confidences. How could he explain his great mistake in refusing the black beast, when no one besides himself knew of the beast's true existence?

There was a tiny photograph beside him where he lay, a flat, duodimensional, black-and-white vision. Melor had first glimpsed this particular photograph nine days ago in this very room. He would never forget that moment in the few living days remaining to him. He had been removing the carefully applied coat of pancake make-up he had worn to a special court function, during which his son, Emperor Matthew I, had awarded him the ceremonial rank of Royal Lord Admiral in gratitude for his services, past and present, in the good interests of the Empire of Man. As he stood before the mirror, wiping his cheeks and forehead, he thought of poor Alyc and how much he regretted his inability to help her. Then the door opened, and Matthew came in.

Perhaps the most difficult aspect of having a son

who was an emperor was the necessity of showing deference to one's own flesh and blood. When Matthew entered the room accompanied by his usual flock of faceless courtiers and scurrying robots, Melor had little choice but to fall to his knees and kiss the imperial signet on Matthew's left index finger.

When that was done, Matthew said, "Please, rise, Father. There's something I feel I ought to show you."

Melor got slowly to his feet. What was particularly odd was that, in Matthew's presence, he felt a true smattering of awe, something that had not affected him on the occasions when he had met alone with Kane IV. But a son was different, he guessed. It was too much like seeing one's younger self garbed in the robes of imperial power. "What is it?" Melor said. He glared at the creatures surrounding his son. "Can't we be alone?"

"Oh, yes, of course. Sorry, Father." Matthew casually waved his retainers out of the room. "This is it here—a photograph."

Melor took the photograph from Matthew's hand, studied it, then shook his head. It was nothing but a view of a section of space, and Melor knew little of space. "Why do you want to show this to me?"

"Well, it is a little strange, isn't it? An astronomer brought it to me. It seems it was just received on a transmission from one of the interstellar research labs. The astronomers were puzzled, so I was informed."

Melor took another look at the photograph. He

stared and squinted and finally realized what he was seeing. When he did, his hands trembled. "Why show me? I know nothing of astronomy. I'm a business-man, a trader. If your astronomers don't know, why should I? Here, take this back."

But Matthew shook his head. "No, you keep it. I've my own copies. I just thought you might be curious."

Melor wasn't curious, but that was only because, of all the men in the Empire, he alone knew exactly what he was seeing. It was a red cloud. A red cloud in the Empire of Man. The black beast had told him about the clouds and, once, shown him photographs. The beast had said the clouds were sent upon the Wykzl as a punishment because they had dared to doubt the power of those mysterious beings the beast claimed to represent. The clouds grew and spread and consumed everything that lay in their path. They can destroy a civilization in time, the beast had said, and the Wykzl will surely be destroyed.

"There's nothing they can do to fight these clouds?" Melor had asked.

"Nothing whatsoever," said the beast, with abso-lute confidence in its own strength.

So, when the Wykzl had asked for aid with which to fight the clouds, Melor had steadfastly refused them.

Now one of the clouds had suddenly appeared within the boundaries of the Empire.

There could be only one explanation: the beast had done it. The beast had told Melor what to do, he had disobeyed, and now he was being punished.

A terrible punishment.

The red cloud might well mean the end not only of the Empire but of the human race.

Had Melor Carey, all by himself, somehow managed to bring about the utter extinction of his own species?

It was not a thought he cared to bear.

But it was true. It must be. The evidence of the photograph testified to that.

"Father, are you ill?" said Matthew, with concern. He reached forward and gripped Melor's frail arms. "Do you want me to call for a medical technician?"

"No, no, I . . . " Melor staggered back toward the softness of his bed. "I'll be all right in a minute. I just . . . "

"It wasn't because of this, was it?" said Matthew, reaching down and retrieving the photograph from the floor where Melor had dropped it.

"No, of course not. I told you that was nothing."

"Then what's wrong?" Casually, Matthew flipped the photograph so that it whirled through the air and landed face-up on the bed beside Melor. "It's not your heart, is it? You last transplant was only two years ago."

"No, it's nothing that serious." Melor kept his eyes turned away from the photograph. "Probably just something I ate—or drank."

"Too much excitement in one day for an old man like you," Matthew said patronizingly.

Melor frowned, but this was no time to assert his

youthful vigor. "Yes, perhaps you're right," he said. "Now please go. I want to be alone. Let me catch my breath, and I'll see you later."

"Of course, Father." Smiling, Matthew went to the door, opened it, and paused. "You needn't bow this time," he said, and went out.

Matthew had left the photograph behind on the bed, but Melor still refused to look at it. Instead, staring at the glittering golden ceiling above, he struggled to arrange his thoughts. Two things disturbed him deeply. The first, the most obvious, was the simple presence of the red cloud. That frightened him, dismayed him, and distressed him. The second thing, more subtle and personal, was Matthew's strange attitude. Why had he shown him the photograph? How could he possibly have guessed its importance? The astronomers knew nothing, and Matthew was nowhere near as smart as they. How had he know the photograph would mean so much to his father?

This suspicion was nothing new. All along, Melor had sensed that something about Matthew was not the same. He had changed too drastically. There was a new confidence, even boldness, that Melor had originally credited simply to the assumption of imperial power. But the more he thought, the more he decided there had to be something more. Matthew carried himself like a man possessed of secret knowledge, as though he knew things Melor could never possibly guess. He finally said the words he had suppressed until now, the words that might explain.

"The black beast," Melor said aloud, and as he did, he was convinced they had to be true.

The black beast, rejected by the father, had gone instead to the son.

Wasn't it even possible that right now, this very moment, as Melor Carey lay alone in his room torn by his own bleak thoughts, Matthew Carey was speaking directly to the black beast?

And so, devastated by these two simultaneous events, the appearance of the red cloud and the treachery of his own son, Melor Carey remained alone in his room for nine days, waiting for death to come and claim him.

In that time, Matthew visited him at least twice daily. On several occasions, indirectly, Melor attempted to raise the subject of the beast, but Matthew always managed skillfully to deflect matters before he could be forced to answer. For Melor, this elusiveness was more suspicious than an outright admission of guilt. He came to believe with fierce certainty that the beast had indeed visited Matthew, and he was equally convinced that the son, unlike the father, would never dare disobey the instructions of that black entity.

Still, it was loneliness that was killing him; it wasn't treachery. If only there had been someone in whom to confide. Speaking strictly, Melor Carey did not want to die, not in the sense of seeking a certain end to life, but there seemed so little choice. When life became a kind of passive death, then the climax of final extinction was a preferable alternative. If his suspicions were correct, then Melor's life had lost the keen rationality it had always possessed, and for him, life without reason was not life at all.

He would have enjoyed explaining his philosophy to another and hearing a response.

But to whom?

Alyc?

He couldn't think of that name without being stricken by terrible, unendurable shame. Hadn't he, to be true, betrayed Alyc in a manner deeper than any Matthew had visited upon him? Months ago, when he'd first reached Earth, he had been apprised of her capture by the space pirates of Quicksilver and, shortly afterward, a crisply worded demand for ransom reached his hands.

He had, of course, ignored it. That first demand and the ones that followed. He knew how wrong he had been. Not only wrong, but mean, cruel, insensitive, and heartless.

Even Matthew had favored meeting the pirates' ransom demands. "There's really no telling what action they might take if we refuse. From all reports, these men lack any glimmering of moral scruples. Buy them off and get Alyc back home where she belongs."

Melor Carey said no. And he was stubborn. A rational man was ruled by his mind, never his emotions. Because he had originally opposed Alyc's trip into space, the consequences of her own decision must lie fully upon her shoulders. She had forced him into a weakened position. How could he, at the very apex of his personal power, stoop to dealing with self-proclaimed pirates?

"They've had her with them for some time now," Melor told Matthew. "Whatever they might want to do to her, I imagine they've already done it."

"But we can't just let them keep her. Like a trophy. A domestic pet."

"Why can't we? What good will she do them? Think, Matthew, use your mind. If we do give them money, what guarantee do we have that they won't instantly demand more? And then what? If it's not money, then it'll be something else. Tools. Arms. Ammunition. A general pardon for all concerned. No, Matthew, I won't be blackmailed. I won't be coerced. I love Alyc more deeply than anything in this universe, but she was warned. My head tells me not to lift a finger. You watch. In the end, bored with her company, the pirates will send her home for free."

Wrong. That was the only word to explain it. Wrong to believe his head and not his heart. When a man began to die, the errors of the past came zinging home, one hurtling dart after another. If only Alyc were here now. He hadn't lied to Matthew: he did love her. Alyc's blindness, for which he blamed himself, had created a natural dependence and, since she was helpless, he had expected and demanded nothing from her. Love between father and daughter was thus made possible. For Matthew, for his son, nothing could be as simple. Melor always remembered his own late father and how well his memory had been served. He expected Matthew to provide for him the same services Melor had rendered his own father.

But now, when he was dying, it was too late. Like most mistakes, this one could never be undone. The pirates had long ago ceased their ransom demands. They turned instead to fomenting rebellion among the backworld planets. Unsuccessfully, to be sure, but this alteration in tactics had served at first only to confirm the rightness of his original decision. The pirates were not merely outlaws, they were rebels, a danger to the imperial order. He knew better now. He wanted Alyc back, had always wanted her back. That was all that mattered—all that could ever matter.

On the sixth day of his illness, he decided to make an effort. When Matthew came to visit, Melor told him, "I have changed my mind about Alyc. I want you to contact these pirates and agree to meet their demands."

Matthew seemed strangely ill-at-ease. "I'm afraid I can't do that, Father," he said softly.

Melor glared. "I don't care what you're the emperor of. She's my daughter and I want it done."

"I didn't say I wouldn't do it, Father. I said I couldn't."

"What do you mean?"

"I mean, I'm sorry to say that further news has

been received. I didn't want to tell you, as ill as you have been, the shock and all . . ."

What frightened Melor was that, despite the surface kindliness of Matthew's words, an underlying current of amused contempt ran through everything he said.

"Just tell me," Melor said. "It's about Alyc, isn't it?"

"Well, yes, sort of. You see, since we agreed not to meet their demands, I had no choice but to regard these pirates as simple rebels. They were, after all, fomenting rebellion within my realm. Several weeks ago I ordered the *Eagleseye* to identify, pursue, and capture these rebels."

"You sent the *Eagleseye* to their homeworld?"

Matthew shook his head. "That, I'm afraid, proved impossible. We still haven't identified where they came from. The *Eagleseye* tracked them down on a desert backworld known as Narabia. The ship went into orbit and set up a heat barrier. The pirates attempted to break free."

"And?" said Melor.

"Their ship was destroyed with all hands aboard."

"Damn, damn, damn!" cried Melor. "Do you mean to tell me that Alyc could be anywhere, with anyone? How dare you—?"

"Wait, Father." Matthew lifted a hand, his left; with the imperial signet. "There's more. After the battle, a party from the *Eagleseye* went down to Narabia and spoke to the natives who had received the pirates. They found that Alyc was among the pirates when they visited the planet and that she was actively aiding their cause."

"I can't believe that."

"It's true, Father. If you wish, I can show you taped testimony. But that's not my point. I don't mean to belittle Alyc at this time. When the pirates left Narabia, when they attempted to break the heat barrier, she went with them. She was killed, Father. Alyc is dead. She was burned alive along with the rest of them."

There was shock. Pain. Horror. Guilt. But not surprise. Melor had known all along that a mistake, once done, could never be easily unraveled. He spoke calmly. "Who ordered the *Eagleseye* to undertake this mission?"

"As I told you, Father, it was I."

"You did this without consulting me, without asking if—"

"You said you would not be coerced. I am the Emperor. I owe certain obligations to my citizens."

"I made you Emperor, Matthew."

"But I rule. And no one—not even you—has the right to question my decisions. I regret Alyc's death as deeply as you. She was my sister. She was also a criminal. Her death was a tragedy, yes, but it was not a mistake."

So he could not confide in Alyc. Alyc was dead.

And Rhisa was dead, too.

He seldom spoke of her, and months went by when he might not even think of her, but he missed her as he missed no one else in the universe, including Alyc.

Rhisa had been gone longer than Alyc.

She was not his wife, not in the strict legal sense, but she was the mother of both Matthew and Alyc. They had lived together secretly for slightly more than four common-years on the family planet, Milrod Eleven. Except for a few submen and robots, no one knew of her existence. Alyc and Matthew had occasionally asked about their mother; Melor told them lies.

He had discovered Rhisa through a careful, scientific survey. As his life passed its hundredth year, he had determined the time had come to obtain a mate. Never doubting exactly what he wanted, physically, intellectually, or spiritually, Melor first had a robot built in the image of his mind's desire. The survey then followed. A hundred agents went to the stars in search of a duplicate match for Melor's robot, and each time one of them returned with a woman, Melor took her into his study where the robot stood and made a quick comparison and, when he found her obviously wanting, sent the woman away.

Rhisa was the one he never sent away.

She came from the planet Tomasis in the nearby Vella Sector and was twenty-two common-years of age. She had pure black hair, impossibly ivory skin, and broad red lips. So did the robot. When she first saw Melor in his study, Rhisa bowed. The robot bowed, too.

"Take off your clothes," he said.

She did so, in a quick easy motion. (The robot also undressed.)

"Turn around—all the way around."

She swiveled on graceful heels. (The robot, too.)

"Speak—say anything."

"I am very proud to make your acquaintance, Mr. Melor Carey." (The robot said, "I am very proud to make your acquaintance, Mr. Melor Carey.")

He hit a button on his desk.

Two servants, submen, entered. "Destroy that," said Melor. He meant the robot. "You, come with me."

She did, to the room that would be hers for the subsequent common-years. Her natural mother and father were made rich. Rhisa bore Melor first a son, then a daughter.

She died.

It happened shortly after the birth of Alyc. Rhisa went out one bright day at dawn to take a walk in the garden. She was bending over, looking at some newly bloomed flowers, when an object—presumably the remnant of a burned-out meteor—dropped from the sky. The object—barely big enough to be seen— struck her shoulder, penetrated the flesh, sliced through her internal organs, and exited through her lower abdomen. Rhisa toppled forward, crushing the flowers she had recently been observing.

She was dead.

Days later, Melor Carey demanded that the odds against such a freak accident be computed. When he received the exact figures, he laughed and laughed.

The number wasn't merely immense. It was impossible. Absurd.

But Rhisa was dead.

He buried her in an unmarked grave exactly at the place where she had died. Later, flowers sprouted there and flourished.

He never mourned her passing.

But he missed her.

That was the strange part, the truth that defied the brute facts. He missed her, because he loved her, and that was so totally unanticipated that it rivaled in terms of absurdity the accident of her death.

Rhisa was like no one he had known in his life. She was always there, as long as he wanted her, an omnipresent force. He couldn't remember when it had started, just that it was early, very early, but he had talked to her. Talked, confided, confessed. He spoke to her of his dreams, hopes, goals, ambitions. He told her everything in his mind and heart, except about the black beast's visits.

She never responded or replied, never said a word unless specifically asked. She was a good woman, an obedient woman according to the established code, but he loved her nonetheless.

In their years together, he doubted they had exchanged a dozen sentences. He talked to her, never with her.

It was a month, two months after her death, when he realized how deeply he missed her. It was late at night, he was alone in his study, he wanted someone to talk to.

There was no one.

She was dead.

Suddenly, he was crying.

That was something he had never done before. Real tears, wet and salty, ran down his ragged face. He couldn't remember crying even as a small child. He wept because the only woman he had ever loved in his life was dead and because, while she was alive, he had never once even faintly recognized the truth of the emotions he felt toward her.

Rhisa was dead. Alyc was dead. Matthew was a traitor.

Melor himself soon would be dead.

On the ninth day of Melor's illness, Matthew came again to visit. He was alone. He found a chair. He sat down. "Feel any better, Father?"

"No."

"Want me to have a medical technician cruise by and take a peek?"

"No."

"Hungry?"

"No."

"Thirsty?"

"No."

"Then—" Matthew stood up, adjusting his

imperial robes "—I'll be back later in the day." Melor said nothing.

Matthew opened the door, went out, was gone.

It would be the same. From this day forward until the official cessation of life. Melor had made up his mind.

Before, for one hundred thirty-two common-years, his life had been composed of a constant succession of achievements. Over and over again, he had won victories, forged ahead, reached goals. He had cried *yes* and *yes* and *yes*, and it was always so.

Now, for the first time, he felt free to cry *no*.

And he intended to say nothing else till the day he gratefully died.

10 AGAINST THE FLEET

Tedric sat in the command chair in the control room of the lead Wykzl cruiser in the rebel attack fleet and watched in wonder as the whirring, beeping, pulsating walls around him operated the ship oblivious to any need for human assistance.

It wasn't the way he would have preferred it; it was the only way it could be done.

Behind, outside the reach of the viewscreen sensors, came another one hundred cruisers almost exactly like this one. Each cruiser carried a single pilot. Phillip Nolan had his own ship. And Keller. And Wilson, the renegade robot. So far, everything was proceeding exactly as planned. The rebel attack force plowed through the barren wastes of N-space. Its destination was imperial Earth. Besides the pirates of Quicksilver, pilots for the fleet had been recruited from the ranks of former sailors among the hundreds who had eagerly stepped forward to volunteer upon the backworld planets. Tedric recalled the scene with some amusement. It had been so different the second time around. The presence of a hundred ready-to-fight attack cruisers had changed a lot of minds, weakened many loyalties. Now the war was on. Even on Narabia, where they had all come so close to dying, the number of men ready to fight and win exceeded the number of ships available to hold them.

Mo-leete, so far, had remained true to his word, which did not necessarily mean that Tedric had discarded all his suspicions. Once Tedric had accepted the original Wykzl offer, all of them had repaired to a neutral sector of space, where soon enough the ships had arrived. As a human pilot was found for each ship, the Wykzl had returned to their own domain. As far as Tedric knew, only two of the aliens—Mo-leete and Ky-shan—remained a part of the rebel force, and even these two had not been permitted to command their own ships. Mo-leete rode with Nolan—as an "observer," he openly claimed—while Ky-shan had agreed to join Keller. Tedric wasn't strictly alone, either. He, in fact, had two passengers aboard his cruiser. Turning in his seat, he spoke to one of them now, "Can you take a look at the navigation panel and give me an estimate when we'll be leaving N-space?"

"Of course, Tedric," said Lady Alyc Carey. "Kisha, would you please?"

"Yes, Alyc," said Kisha. She crossed the room to one of the flashing wall panels, glanced down with practiced ease, and returned to whisper in Alyc's ear.

"She says it'll be thirty-seven common-minutes," said Alyc.

Tedric nodded. The tension he felt made talking difficult. "It's not going to be easy after that."

"I never thought it would be."

"As the lead ship, we're sure to catch hell. Once we reach the Solar System, it'll be another five or ten minutes before the next ship can decelerate sufficiently to join us. For that amount of time, we're going to have to take everything they throw at us and hope we won't be burned alive. Surprise is the one factor in our favor. The imperial fleet doesn't know when or exactly where we'll appear. But they'll find us. You can bet on that. It might take a minute or two or three, but we won't get out of this without taking a lot of heat."

"Tedric, I know all that," Alyc said.

He laughed, understanding, as did she, that the same tension that had kept him from talking was now causing him to talk too much. Still, he knew he was right. The imperial fleet would be ready for them. Several minor skirmishes had already been fought out among the backworlds. The fleet had a pretty fair idea of the size of the rebel force massing for attack and an equally fair idea that it wouldn't wait long to move. Naturally, it had not proved possible to keep their recruitment drive secret. There was no way to gather up a hundred pilots from a dozen worlds without arousing someone's interest. The *Eagleseye* had never shown its bloated mass—back to Earth, Tedric guessed—but a number of other imperial cruisers had. No effort had been made by the rebels to disguise their basic objective: an attack on Earth designed to destroy the fleet and overthrow Matthew I. Tedric's ship was specifically equipped with Wykzl shields designed to bear the brunt of the initial imperial counterattack. Still, he was worried. He wished they'd hurry up and reach their destination. Then there wouldn't be time to think anymore.

Suddenly, from one of the rear control panels, a shrill siren began to wail.

Tedric swung his chair, wishing, not for the first time, that these ships were not quite so automatic and that a pilot could identify a problem by simply asking.

Still, he didn't have to wonder for long. As he turned, his gaze crossed the forward viewscreen, and he saw the problem there. It seemed impossible, and he had to stare. A ship. An imperial ship. A reconnaissance cruiser. And it was coming straight toward them.

Tedric cursed softly, but that would have no helpful effect. The Wykzl ship itself—its computer, actually—had seen the intruding imperial cruiser and was prepared to take action. Tedric fully realized, whatever he chose to do now, it was too late to save himself. Even as he first saw it, the imperial cruiser had undoubtedly been eagerly transmitting, contacting its distant headquarters and describing exactly what it had found in the emptiness of N-space: Tedric's approaching cruiser.

As Tedric watched, the reconnaissance cruiser began a maneuver intended to turn it around. For a long moment, he simply observed, receiving a sort of sensual delight from the sight of such graceful ease. Then he let the anger and frustration he felt take control of his fingers. There were two sets of buttons located in the padded arms of his command chair. He punched the set to his left. They meant only one thing: a message to the ship: the intruder is an enemy: open fire.

The ship itself proceeded from there. Tedric crossed his arms and waited. Alyc said something which sounded like, "Are you going to kill them?" He didn't know. The decision was out of his hands. The ship would have to decide.

A pair of matching blue bolts, as straight as a surveyor's line, sliced through the void. Tractor beams. Because of its defensive capabilities, Tedric's ship was not heavily armed, but the reconnaissance vessel would likely be even less so. The tractor beams caught the enemy ship partway through its turning maneuver and held it fast, like the fibers of an insect's web. So swiftly that Tedric could not follow, a burst of yellow fire came next. The heatray. The suddenness of the assault appeared to catch the enemy ship unaware. There was never time to lift a defensive shield. The heatray struck the unprotected hull and easily penetrated. It was over in a moment. There was no sound, no explosion, no sudden puff. The reconnaissance cruiser simply disappeared. It was there—in space—and then it was no longer there. Briefly, with nothing to hold, the tractor beams clutched fitfully at the void. Then they withdrew. The pure gray of N-space flowed without interruption. Life had come, enclosed in a fragile ship, gone, and left no sign.

Tedric realized that, all this time, he had been holding his breath in his lungs. He let it escape in a great whoosh.

"They—they are gone," said Kisha.

"No, they're dead," Alyc softly corrected.

Tedric knew he should say something too, but words failed him. Despite the battles he had fought before, despite the warrior past he glimpsed in dreams, he did not enjoy killing; it wasn't his nature to take a life. If he could have done it without thinking later, he might have endured it better. But he couldn't. Still, the crucial factor had to be the matter of time: later. He would have to worry about the killing then; he couldn't do it now. "They saw us," he said, "which means the imperial fleet will know. They won't know where we'll be coming, but they'll have a good idea when."

From her expression, it was plain that Alyc hadn't paused from her worry about the killing to consider what else the appearance of the reconnaissance ship might mean. "What should we do? Stop? Turn back?"

"No, that's impossible. We've come too far."

"Should we tell the others?"

"No, not that either. I don't want to break radio

silence, and there's nothing anyone could do. It was pure luck—their good and our bad. N-space is infinite, supposedly, which means locating us was as likely as finding the one good egg in a mountain of bad ones. But they did it."

"We can still hold out."

"I suppose so."

Kisha, unusually active, had gone to the navigation panel again. "We have only twelve minutes to decide," she said, ignoring Tedric, as always, and speaking to Alyc.

But he heard, too. "Then cross your fingers," he said.

Alyc looked puzzled. "Why? What will that do?"

"I understand it helps the gods decide to join our side."

Alyc nodded and held up both hands. The fingers were neatly crossed. "Like this?"

Tedric nodded. "Yes, exactly."

Then he crossed his own fingers. Both hands, too.

Phillip Nolan sat poised in the command chair of his attack cruiser and gazed at the viewscreens around his head that showed a panoramic view of the hurtling rebel fleet.

"What's the time, Mo-leete?" he asked the Wykzl, who shared the control room with him.

Mo-leete stood beside the navigation panel. "Eighteen minutes, fifteen seconds."

"Is that for us or them?"

"Only for us, friend Nolan."

He calculated quickly. "Then Tedric and Alyc should be entering the Solar System and encountering the imperial fleet in about eight minutes."

"The battle will commence then."

"And we won't know about it."

"We will when we arrive."

"Sure." It was meaningless chatter—designed to fill the time. Eighteen minutes of time according to the universally accepted constant of Earth's rotation. Closer to seventeen by now—the chatter itself had lopped off that many seconds.

"Any other information you require?" asked Mo-leete.

"No, I can handle it."

"Then I will observe." Mo-leete went back to his chair and sat down. Nolan appreciated the scrupulous caution Mo-leete was showing, but that was only right and proper. Despite the invaluable assistance the Wykzl had provided, this was mankind's war and had to remain so. It had to be fought hand-to-hand without the intrusion of any blue paws. Mo-leete had actively intervened only once, about twenty minutes ago. From his place close to the radio panel, he had noticed an odd burst of activity. Since the rebel fleet maintained a discreet radio silence and the signal came from nearby, Mo-leete couldn't understand it. Nolan told Mo-leete to try to find the transmitting band, but the activity ceased before he could locate it.

For a time after that, there was nothing, then only a few minutes ago, there was another burst of activity. This was even more puzzling than the first, since it wasn't a radio signal. The activity seemed to emanate from close ahead. Mo-leete had the ship compute a specific point. Still, when they passed that point, there was nothing to be seen.

"So much for that problem," Nolan said.

Mo-leete seemed less sure. "I almost feared the presence of an intruder."

"An imperial ship?"

"It might have come across Tedric's lead cruiser."

"But that doesn't seem possible. N-space is so vast."

"In an infinite universe, where an infinite number of possibilites exist, there can be no such thing as an impossibility."

"That sounds like alien philosophy to me."

"But you are the alien, friend Nolan, not I."

Nolan laughed, but his heart wasn't in it. Not then, and not now. His heart didn't have the strength to do much of anything, except pound, and beat, and maybe squat in his mouth. Nolan was scared, and he knew he was scared, but that didn't make it any easier to bear. He had experienced battle only once before and that time, on Evron Eleven against the Wykzl cruiser, there hadn't been enough time to get scared. He thought he would be all right once the fighting started. The gleam of tractor beams and the blaze of heatrays. But even knowing that did not make the present ordeal of waiting any more bearable.

"I believe it is now time," Mo-leete suddenly said.

Nolan came out of his private ruminations. "For Tedric?"

"He should be appearing in normal space about now."

Nolan shook his head, because there was really nothing he could say or do. His ears were alert, as if the sounds of distant battle might somehow reach them, but that, of course, was impossible, even in a universe of infinite possibilities. "Mo-leete," said Nolan, "there's something I've wondered about: do you or your people have much truck with the concept of a supreme cosmic being?"

Mo-leete gave an exaggerated shrug. "At times we do and at times we do not. Why do you ask, friend Nolan?"

"Because I was thinking how, if you did and if I did, then maybe we could do something nice and ask him to intervene on our side in this upcoming battle."

"You mean pray?"

"Yes, something like that."

"But would such a being, if it did in fact exist, stoop so low as to interfere in our petty struggles?"

Nolan stroked his chin with what he hoped would appear sagacity. "For my own self, no, I doubt it." He grinned. "But it wouldn't hurt to ask anyway, would it?"

Mo-leete smiled, too. It was an odd sort of a

smile, because Mo-leete's teeth, even though he possessed a complete mouthful, followed no regular pattern; there were unexpected gaps and crazy patterns that broke the usual symmetry. "No, friend Nolan, I doubt that even God could harm us now."

On his cruiser, an anonymous component within the rebel fleet, Wilson the renegade robot sat and brooded. He couldn't help himself, because his mind always beat at such a fantastic rate, and there was really nothing else to do at this time except think.

His thoughts ran as follows: Since I'm a robot and the rest of them are human beings, I'm probably a damned fool for getting mixed up in their petty problems. Hell, I'm a freak of nature as well as a child of man, and the fact that I happened to emerge from the laboratory vats with a heart and emotions as well as a good, keen mind is something nobody has ever satisfactorily explained. Still, whatever I've got that other robots do not, I'm no human being. In the classical sense, I'm more human than ninety percent of them, but with no mother or father in any sort of sense, I know I'll never be accepted as one of them. I like Tedric. Even Nolan, with his faults and family, can be fun. It's not the individuals I have problems with: it's the race—the whole damned human species. The Dynarx, as usual, have the right perspective. If everything's chaos, then ride with the storm. If nothing has any particular point or purpose, then everything's of equal value. I'm more like one of those green alien slimy slugs than I am any human being. I've got arms and legs, a chin and nostrils, hair and knuckles, but that's all camouflage. What's important is hidden underneath and that's wire, steel, complex circuitry. I'm an outlaw. I can't change, because I was born that way. Maybe, like now, I'll stand beside them. Maybe, like now, I'll say their cause is the same as my own. But that's camouflage, too. The truth is I'm Wilson the renegade robot. And that's because I'm too damned human to be anything else.

He glanced at the ship's navigation panel, sharp eyes picking up the tiny flickering figures even at this distance. The time was slightly more than nine minutes, which meant that Tedric, in command of the lead cruiser in the rebel fleet, ought to have entered the Solar System one full minute ago. In other words, even as Wilson sat brooding over his own contrary thoughts, the battle itself was raging. Hang on, Wilson found himself thinking. Hang on, Tedric, and take whatever they dish out. The rest of us are coming, a hundred strong. Hang on and we'll catch them and hold them and proceed to whip the hell out of them.

His own fervor surprised him. Suddenly, Wilson grinned and threw up his arms. "Hell," he said aloud, "what's the purpose of having a philosophy except to teach a person to care?"

For the subman Keller, the rebellion against Emperor Matthew I had come to resemble a very private holy war. Victory for him meant much more than a shift in the identity of those who gripped the reigns of imperial power. It had to mean more than that. It had to mean freedom and had to mean liberation. Keller had not discussed his views with anyone else; he had received no official sanction of any kind. But he believed what he felt. If he had not, he would have immediately taken the cruiser he commanded and turned it around and refused to proceed one kilometer farther. He didn't do that. It meant he believed.

Keller had a wife. Her name was Jania and she lived on a world known as Evron Eleven. Keller himself had lived on the planet for some time, but he had gone away, and Jania could never do that. Both of them had been brought to Evron Eleven while they were still children. Because slavery had been outlawed throughout the Empire of Man since its inception as a political unit, they were not called slaves. They were workers, and they were paid a set salary to dig Dalkanium in the deep mines, but since their salaries could never equal the price of passage away from Evron Eleven, then what else were they except slaves —slaves without the comfort of an owner's responsibility?

Their parents had sold them to the Carey family interests who operated the mines on Evron Eleven. That was never a pleasant subject to think about, because Keller recalled his parents—and Jania's, too— as good, kind, generous people, but they were also poor and often hungry, and he could never be sure whether he should hate them because of what they had done or simply pity them.

A subman was not a human being, and that was the key proposition. There were no human beings in the mines of Evron Eleven, except a few paid supervisors, and there never could be. Despite centuries of interbreeding, the distinction between the races remained plain for anyone with eyes to see. The submen were descended from the products of various experiments conducted on pre-imperial Earth in an attempt to add certain human characteristics, primarily intelligence, to the genetic make-up of Earth's ancient animal species. Keller, himself, or so he understood, owed much of his genetic heritage to a now extinct domestic pet called a dog. But a dog walked on four legs, and Keller used only two. A dog couldn't talk, and Keller could. A dog couldn't conceive of the future in terms of present predictable phenomena, and Keller could. He felt he was human. He considered himself to be a man, and so did every other subman he had ever met. But the humans themselves didn't feel that way, and they never hesitated to buy and sell submen, treat them like slaves without calling them that. What their ancestors had made, they still owned. It made him ill. It made him sick with anger and resentment and frustration. What made it worse, until now, was his personal helplessness: there was nothing he could do to change what was.

After he and Jania came to Evron Eleven, they were sent below into the mines and years passed and he never saw the sun above. In darkness, he worked, knowing full well that the only result of his labor would be riches for the Careys and eventual death for himself. That was why when the recruiters came and said that any physically able male who wished to enlist as a sailor in the imperial navy would be accepted for immediate duty, he raised his hand. Jania, of course, could not. The established code of feminine conduct prevented her. And he had gone away. She had remained behind. She had never fully forgiven him for what he had done.

Jania, in spite of the odds, was still alive. He had seen her not long ago, for the first time since his departure, when the giant cruiser on which he served, the *Eagleseye*, had been ordered to Evron Eleven to crush a rebellion among the workers there. He and Tedric and Phillip Nolan had been captured by the rebels. Jania was one of their leaders. Although at first she refused to recognize him, a reconciliation of sorts had been worked out. Still, when it came time for the *Eagleseye* to depart for Earth, Jania was forced to stay behind. She would return to the mines. And he could not bear that. There was nothing he could do, but he could no longer stand to do nothing. Would this present rebellion make any difference? The rebel fleet, whose members came largely from the backworld planets where few submen lived, was a human fleet. Would Prince Randow, if he assumed the throne, act any differently than Emperor Matthew? To be honest, Keller did not know. Yet despite this, he chose to believe. He felt he had no alternative. For him, nothing else mattered except the liberation of his species. He refused to take any action that did not assist in making that dream a reality.

He was not alone aboard this cruiser. Ky-shan, the Wykzl, rode with him, and even though Keller still felt less than comfortable in the alien's company, he had long ago learned to tolerate him, and they got on politely. Ky-shan, at Tedric's instruction, took no active role in the ship's operation, but he did keep Keller informed of their progress. Now, interrupting Keller's thoughts, Ky-shan said, "According to my calculations, we should enter the Solar System in five minutes."

Keller looked up, caught by genuine surprise. "Are you sure about that?"

"The navigation panel so states, friend Keller."

He knew he couldn't disagree with that. The figure impressed him. Five minutes meant that the lead ship, with Tedric aboard, had entered normal space three minutes before. The battle—for whatever purpose—was on.

"Better give everything a final going over," he told Ky-shan, forgetting for the moment that the Wykzl was not supposed to be an active participant in the impending battle. "Check the shields and rays. Once we come out, there may not be time."

"But we will win," Ky-shan said, with surety.

"We will?" Even Keller was not that convinced.

"Yes, naturally."

"How do you know for sure?"

"Because if we do not, we will be dead, and if we are dead, then we will never know, and if we never know we have lost, then how can it be truly said that we have lost?"

Keller couldn't argue with the impeccable logic of the Wykzl. *When we win, you'll be free.* He thought that, but didn't say it. The pledge was a private one—to Jania.

Then Keller set about preparing for the battle that lay ahead.

Tedric faced pure hell, and there was nothing he could do. The imperial fleet fired bolt after bolt of heat at his lone ship, and somehow he withstood it. The calendar clicked off the passing seconds till help might arrive. There might be enough of them, and there might not. There was nothing he could do until they came.

The situation had developed much as he might have predicted—and feared. The reconnaissance ship had alerted the imperial fleet of his approach, and Matthew Carey, no fool to be sure, had stationed his cruisers in a ring at the ecliptic just beyond the orbit of Pluto. Because of this, as soon as Tedric emerged from N-space, a half-dozen blazing cruisers were instantly upon him. He raised his shields, made no effort to fight back, and kept his fingers crossed. That was four minutes ago. He had six more to endure. He still didn't know whether it would prove too many.

Carey had only two strategic choices. He could

either concentrate the entirety of his fleet upon the first intruding vessel—with Tedric aboard—or else he could hold back the bulk of his forces until the arrival of the remainder of the fleet.

Tedric's own preferences in this matter were dangerously ambiguous. If the entire imperial fleet came against him, then the chances of his ship surviving very long were severely limited. Still, if he held out and kept the fleet closely engaged, then it might give time for the rebel forces to appear and form their own encircling ring around the clustered imperial cruisers. If, instead, the bulk of the fleet remained spread out, he might very well live through these first ten isolated minutes, but the chances for ultimate victory by the rebel fleet would be considerably lessened.

Officially, Tedric had to hope that Carey selected the first option. Personally—and especially with Alyc aboard—he couldn't help wishing for the second. Carey had apparently decided to take the first route. From the amount of heat his shields received, Tedric estimated at least three dozen cruisers were firing at him. The imperial fleet, in its entirety, numbered no more than forty available cruisers. On the viewscreens above his head, Tedric counted the hulls of twenty-seven nearby ships. Most of these were not large, though at least twice the size of his Wykzl ship, but one was particularly huge: his old companion, the *Eagleseye*, he guessed. Tedric would have bet anything that Emperor Matthew himself was aboard that ship.

So, while Carey's decision might well have cost

Tedric the battle, it might also have won the war for the rebel side. Still, with death staring so near, it was hard for Tedric to concentrate upon the triumph that might come later.

Alyc did not appear disturbed. Part of this was ignorance—Tedric had seen no reason to enlighten her concerning the options her brother faced—but another part was sheer courage. It was already getting warm inside the control room. Tedric loosened his shirt and tried not to perspire. The heat itself meant nothing. There was no way they could live long enough to die from the heat. The ship would burn up long before; the shields would fall.

Alyc waved her hands helplessly. "Tedric, isn't there anything else we can do? It seems so senseless just to sit here and wait for them to destroy us."

She could not, of course, see how bad their situation was but, as often happened with her, she seemed to know without the assistance of her eyes. He said, "We could try to fight them, but there wouldn't be much point. There's too many of them and too few of us. I counted twenty-seven cruisers in the screens and there's more outside the range of our sensors. I doubt that the heatray on this ship is powerful enough to penetrate their shields. If I took a shot at them, I'd just be wasting energy."

"Then we have to stay here, trapped?"

"Until the others arrive, I'm afraid so."

"And when will that be?"

Tedric didn't have to look at the navigation panel

to tell her. By now, he could feel the passing seconds as they slipped by: "About four minutes."

"Will we make it that long?"

He told her the truth: "I don't know."

Except for the growing heat, there was little outward indication of their plight. The ship didn't rock or sway. There was no sensation of being under fire. Death, when it came, would no doubt catch them unaware. A sudden *poof*, a rush of utter cold and hellish heat, and it would be over.

Tedric paced the length of the control room. He paused briefly, inspecting a few of the less important panels, then came back. Standing in front of Alyc's chair, he said, "We might just make it. We really might."

Alyc turned her head, as if seeking him out, and said, with all sincerity, "And if we do not?"

That was the last possibility Tedric wished to consider at this time, but her honesty deserved something similar in return. The heat in the room was growing close to unbearable, but Alyc seemed unaffected. "Then I'll be very sorry," he told her. "And I don't just mean that for myself—for you, too. I was the one who thought it was safe enough to bring you here. I should have made you ride on another ship. If I was wrong, then I've got a lot to feel sorry for."

"If it doesn't matter to me, Tedric, why should it matter to you?"

"Because it should matter to you. There's no good reason for you to die this soon."

"But I'm blind. A cripple. I enjoy being here with

you. I want to be here. There's really no other place for me."

This was the closest Alyc had ever come to declaring an ultimate shift in loyalties. He knew he could press her further and perhaps get her to denounce her father and brother. He wouldn't do that. It was the same here as back on Narabia. Any time, he might call the *Eagleseye* and force Alyc in front of the screen and show her to them and say, "Here, look, do you really want to kill this girl?" It might save not only her life but his as well. But he couldn't do it. For her sake, he wished he could, but didn't her trust and loyalty deserve something equal in kind?

Turning, Tedric peered across the room toward the navigation panel. The figures were easy to read. He calculated half-consciously. Two minutes, four-teen seconds. What would they do? All along, he had expected that the imperial fleet would eventually choose to withdraw and wait for the arrival of the bulk of the rebel ships, but time was growing short—a fact that the enemy must realize, too—and the feroc-ity of their attack had in no way lessened.

Tedric tasted the salty sweat upon his lips. Kisha, with her coat of fur, breathed slowly and heavily. Only Alyc remained untouched. Like a pillar of ice, she loomed above the barren polar wastes.

Aboard his command ship, the imperial fleet cruiser *Eagleseye,* Emperor Matthew I repeated his order and cursed those men who had so far failed to carry it out. "I want that ship destroyed," he cried out.

"I want it reduced to ashes, and I don't care how many ships or how much energy it takes to bring that about."

The primary recipient of his anger was an old acquaintance, Captain John Maillard, commander of the *Eagleseye,* whom Matthew refused to trust. But Maillard was the best tactician in the entire navy, and trust at the moment was a far less essential commodity than competency. Maillard said, "It must be their shields. They're a Wykzl device, and we frankly haven't the slightest idea what sort of technological advances the Wykzl might have made in the hundred years since the end of the war. Whatever it is, they're good. Any shields known to man would have fallen five minutes ago under the sort of attack we've launched on that ship."

"Then launch something stronger," said Matthew, but the force in his voice had weakened. Except for the usual robot technicians, he and Maillard were now alone in the ship's cramped control room. There was no one to impress with the strength of his authority.

"We have nothing stronger," Maillard said. "It's possible, of course, that the cumulative power of our attack may break their shields at any time, but personally I would recommend withdrawal. The bulk of their fleet is due to appear soon. When they do, we don't want to be caught with our own forces concentrated."

Matthew knew all about the strategic options involved, but what Maillard didn't know was why the destruction of this one rebel ship was so crucial. Nor could Matthew enlighten him. It was the black beast. The black beast had appeared before Emperor Matthew and said, "You must concentrate your fire upon the first of the rebel ships to appear. This ship will be piloted by the one man among the rebels who presents a true threat to your reign. His name is Tedric. Kill him, destroy his ship, and victory will be yours."

But why? Matthew knew this man Tedric. He was undoubtedly a strange one, a mystery man whose origins were clouded in doubt, but why should he present such a dangerous threat? Matthew had asked the black beast for an explanation and been told that none was necessary. He didn't know about the truth of that, but he was beginning to worry. If Tedric was a threat, whom did he threaten? Was it Matthew and his reign, or was it perhaps the black beast itself?

Still, he had not yet reached the point where he dared disobey the advice he received. The beast had told him about Melor Carey and the red cloud and what happened to a man when he dared to act contrary to what he was told. Softly, Matthew told Captain Maillard, "Proceed with the present attack. If the rebel fleet appears, then we'll withdraw."

"There won't be time," Maillard said flatly.

"Then make time!" Matthew cried angrily. "I won't have my orders questioned. I am the Emperor! You wouldn't have argued with that fool, Kane. Don't do it with me!"

"Yes, your highness," Maillard said, with a hint of mockery in his tone. He went to the robots and relayed the instructions he had received from his emperor.

Matthew shut his eyes. There was nothing more to see, nothing more to do. He had asserted his own identity: he alone was the Emperor Matthew I.

But was that true?

Even with his eyes shut, Matthew could see the dark looming form of the black beast. Except, this time, it refused to utter a word.

It seemed to be laughing at him.

In the imperial palace on New Melbourne on the planet Earth, Melor Carey finally shut his eyes.

All this day and all of the past night, he had lain with his eyes no more than half open. They brought him vague, flickering, uncertain images of an occasionally bright, sometimes dark world beyond his own mind. With his eyes shut, the uncertainty vanished, and now he saw clearly for the first time. He saw a green world filled with trees and flowers. There was a great house, a beaming sun in the sky, a blue zigzagging brook.

He knew he was home. This was Milrod Eleven he was seeing.

And as well as he saw that, Melor Carey also knew that he would never see that place again.

Melor Carey was dying here on Earth. He would never leave this bed alive.

"Matthew," he whispered hoarsely. "Alyc."

He was alone. Carefully, he searched back through his memory to determine where the others had gone. Alyc, he recalled first, had been taken forceably from him by some men known as the space pirates of Quicksilver. He knew he would never see her again, but there was only a faint sensation of regret; except for the nature of her fate, he had forgotten Alyc. If she entered the room right now and somehow got him to open his heavy eyes, he knew he would never recognize her.

Matthew's fate was more complex—and also more distinctly familiar. Melor knew he had seen his son only lately. He could not specifically recall where or when, but it was neither long ago nor far away. Dimly, through a fog, he recalled something about a war, a battle. He recalled that his son, like his daughter, had been taken from him. The black beast had done it. He remembered the beast.

And then it appeared to him.

Even now, in the final languid phase of his life, Melor Carey knew enough to recognize that this could not be real. His eyes were closed and his world was dark, but there stood the beast.

Melor spoke calmly, with the total dignity of a man left wholly to himself. "What do you want here with me?"

"I speak for those I represent," said the beast.

"Then speak." Melor could not hear his own voice, but the words of the beast reached him clearly.

"I have instructions for you."

"Then speak them."

"Melor, you must live," said the beast. "Those I represent demand this of you."

He laughed. It was a painful gesture, and his whole body burned with hellish agony, but how could he stop himself? For all these years, the beast had visited him, conveying advice, instructions, and orders, and all these years, he had obeyed. But what now? What was left? Now it came to him and said he must live, but the point wasn't that he would not live but that he could not. The beast had met its match at last, and if that match wasn't Melor himself, then at least it was death—his own death. And he went on laughing.

"Shut up!" the beast cried frantically. "How dare you laugh at me! Shut your mouth, you stupid old man!"

And Melor sat up. His eyes remained shut, but an incredible strength flowed through him and he rose with the ease of a feather. He lifted a finger and pointed it blindly at the beast. "No, not me," he cried, "you! You shut up! You go away! The human race has no more need of your kind. Get out! Be gone from my sight! Be—!"

Melor halted in mid-sentence. His strength gave out with the suddenness of an explosion. He fell back. He no longer moved.

Shortly afterward, when the robot medical technician entered the dark room to inspect its patient, all it found was a dead old man.

Melor Carey.

The room was empty.

There was no black beast to be seen.

Unable to control his joy, Tedric leaped up and down in the middle of the floor, waving his arms. He reached out and grabbed Alyc and hugged her and planted a wet kiss on her cheek. He reached out and grabbed Kisha and hoisted her in the air and spun her around until even she was laughing.

The viewscreens told the story. The crowded, packed, cluttered viewscreens. Ship after ship after ship. Rebel ships! His ships! And these ships had the imperial fleet surrounded.

"Fire!" cried Tedric. "Keep firing till you burn every one of them to ash. Fire and fire and fire!" Letting go of Kisha, he turned and hurried to one of the forward panels. The defensive shields that protected the ship remained intact, but they no longer faced the furious assault of the previous minutes. Tedric hit two levers. He wanted to fire. His face jerked upward toward the nearest viewscreen and he saw the twin yellow beams of the heatrays come lashing out from the belly of his own ship. He didn't care if they struck home. With a hundred ships on the attack, his own petty offensive capabilities could make little difference. But he wanted to help. He wanted to pay them back for all he had endured. Grabbing the controls, he directed the beams toward the *Eagleseye*. He knew they would have little effect against the shields of that mighty ship. Still, he didn't care. Matthew Carey was aboard the *Eagleseye*, and it was Carey he wanted to strike now.

"Tedric." There was a gentle hand on his shoulder. Turning, he found Alyc gazing sightlessly up at him.

"Yes?" he said in a tone at odds with his previous excitement.

"Tedric, tell me what is happening. I can't see. Please tell me."

He let the heatrays alone and spoke to her. "It was really very simple, Alyc. We couldn't have worked it better if we'd planned it. Carey simply didn't give up. As long as we sat here, he sent every ship in his fleet against us. Don't tell me how we held out as long as we did, but the fact is we made it, and that's all that's important. Now the fleet's come. Our fleet. With Carey's forces concentrated around us, it was easy enough to outmaneuver them and form a circle. Their energies are depleted. Their rays are weak and their shields are thin. We've got a hundred ships to their forty and we're beating the hell out of them. Look! See it there!" He waved at one of the screens. "There's one of them burning now!"

"Then we've won," she said.

He sat down. The calmness in her voice was catching. "We have. Or we will. It's not entirely over yet, but we've got them beat. What ever made Carey do what he did was a mistake. He couldn't know we were aboard. It was just dumb. It makes no sense."

"Then call them," she said.

"Call? Call who?"

"Why, the others of course. Wilson and Phillip and the rest. Shouldn't Matthew be given an opportunity to surrender? If he's beaten as badly as you say, then there's no point in carrying on the slaughter."

Tedric had to admit that she was right. Even while she spoke, above his head, two more members of the imperial fleet winked out of existence. Two times twenty or thirty crew members. It was a slaughter. He reached for the radio. "I'll do that."

But in the end there proved to be no need. Before his hand could touch the phone, the firing in the viewscreens suddenly ceased. Carey had surrendered. There had been no need for anyone to ask. He might be stupid, but he was not a fool.

Then the suddenness of victory overwhelmed Tedric. There was nothing else he could do. All these months, he had struggled to attain this end, and now that it had at last been won, he couldn't help asking himself the only questions that might at this time have disturbed him.

What now? What next?

Alyc was looking at him. Whether she could see him or not, it didn't matter; she was looking at him. She said, "It's got to be better. My father was wrong and Matthew was wrong. I understand that. So it's got to be better now."

He nodded his head, a private gesture. He hoped she was right, but for better or worse, he alone fully understood how much remained to be done. There were the red clouds, for instance, and even that might be no more than a beginning. "Do your voices tell you anything?" he asked her.

She shook her head. "Not them. I think it's my heart that does."

It was melodramatic but he didn't laugh. Perhaps his heart sometimes talked, too.

The radio was flashing. Tedric reached for the receiver and punched it to life. Above his head, in the center viewscreen, Phillip Nolan's grinning face appeared.

"Carey's thrown in the towel," he said. "You beat him damn near singlehandedly, Tedric. All the rest of us did was come along and sweep up the broken pieces."

Tedric smiled faintly. "Where do we go now?"

"To Earth. New Melbourne. Our next step is to take control of the palace and release poor Prince Randow from whatever jail he inhabits."

"What about Carey?"

"He's been ordered to proceed alone. Just the *Eagleseye*. Captain Maillard's aboard and he's agreed to keep an eye on Carey. The rest of the imperial fleet —there's twenty or so ships undestroyed—will remain out here under guard."

"Then I'll meet you on Earth," Tedric said. "Bring a bundle of roses when you come."

"I'll try."

Tedric shut off the radio and turned back to Alyc and, when he did, saw that she was crying. He moved to console her, and Kisha, who had also moved forward, stepped back and let him.

What was odd was that, even though he did not fully comprehend the reasons for her tears, he felt almost as if he ought to join her.

11 BEATING THE ODDS

On the home planet of the Carey family, Milrod Eleven, Tedric and the Lady Alyc strolled languidly through the lush thicket of the garden that lay behind the main house. It was mid-afternoon in this part of the otherwise uninhabited planet, and the sun pounded mercilessly down upon both their bare heads. Alyc wore a blue silk gown that just missed sweeping the bare ground, while Tedric was dressed in the silver uniform of the Imperial Corps of the One Hundred. On the collar of his shirt were a pair of matching oak leaf clusters. Prince Randow—now Emperor Randow II—had asked Tedric, in the first glow of victory, to assume command of the entire Corps. He had refused that offer, suggesting an alternative, but had agreed to accept an immediate promotion to the rank of major. He was here today because Alyc had invited him. Her message, reaching him on Earth, claimed that it was vitally important that she see him at once. So far, she had made no reference to that message, but he did not greatly mind. He would have accepted her invitation in any event, whether imperative or not.

She said, "So you don't think you can stay for more than one day."

He shook his head, forgetting as he often did that she could not see. "I shouldn't." The grace with which she glided down the narrow garden paths astonished him. There was not the merest hint of her handicap. Here in her own home, Alyc was master. She exuded confidence as well as grace. He said, "Milrod Eleven was on my way, so to speak, and since it was important, I thought I ought to stop."

"I'm glad I was convenient."

"And I did want to say good-bye before I left for good."

"You sound almost as if you won't be coming back."

He nodded, another forgetful gesture. "It may be a time. This isn't an easy mission."

"No, I suppose not."

He found himself speaking with surprising freeness. The words flowed. He might have been a young boy describing distant half-seen dreams. "You saw the cloud that Mo-leete showed us. There's no greater mystery in the Galaxy today. I haven't the slightest idea what it means. Neither does anyone else. Somebody's got to go out there. I thought it should be me."

"Does it present an immediate danger?"

"No, not really. There are no inhabited worlds in that sector."

"Then couldn't you have waited?"

She knew him so well. The truth, as Alyc apparently guessed, was that after six common-months of inactivity at the new imperial court on Earth, Tedric had leaped at the opportunity to be away. Yes, the red cloud might have waited, but Tedric himself could not. "I didn't see any reason for waiting."

"No, I'm sure you didn't." She was smiling—with him more than at him. "And you will have help?"

"Ky-shan has some familiarity with the clouds. I'll be glad to have him along."

"It's too bad he couldn't have come down with you."

"Well, there was work for him aboard the cruiser."

Naturally, that wasn't true. Ky-shan had remained aboard ship, one of the cruisers borrowed from the Wykzl, in orbit around Milrod Eleven. He could have joined Tedric in the shuttle heading below. But Tedric had wanted to see Alyc alone. He didn't tell her that—it wouldn't have been proper—but he was sure that she knew.

"But what about the others? Like most victims, I'm curious about the fate of my kidnappers. You said Keller had gone back to Evron Eleven."

"Prince Randow issued an order—I'm afraid

Phillip and I had to push him a little—freeing the submen from Carey family contracts. Keller is a member of the Corps now. We gave him a combat commission. We also gave him leave to go fetch Jania. It meant a lot to him. He actually wept when we told him."

"He might be in love with her."

Tedric felt oddly embarrassed. "Yes, I suppose he is."

"Let's sit here."

They had come to a break in the foliage, a small cleared space with a shallow pond. There were two narrow wooden benches. Without needing to look, Alyc sat down upon one of them. Facing her, Tedric sat upon the other. "As for Phillip," he said, "the last I heard he's still at home with his father and brothers."

"And he's the new commander of the Corps."

"Randow offered him the position, and he accepted."

"After you had refused."

He had no idea how she knew about that, but she was right. "He's unencumbered. He'll do a better job than I could."

She laughed, high and shrill, like a happy bird. "I think you just couldn't stand the idea of sitting still. I know who you are, Tedric. I know what you need in order to live."

"Well, there are other things for me to do besides signing my name all day."

"You've got to fight, Tedric. You've got to always be moving."

He stared wistfully at the quiet garden surrounding him. "I think I could endure a world like this for a time, Alyc."

She nodded. "For a time, yes. A short time. It grows tiring, Tedric. I live here. I've hardly ever known anything else, and I ought to know. One grows weary, Tedric. It's too passive, motionless, stationary. It just sits here. Life can't be like that."

"Maybe it ought to be."

"But it isn't. Here's somebody I want you to meet."

He had to put it down to her keen sense of hearing. He looked up but saw no one in sight. It was several further moments before he heard the crackle of footsteps advancing through the bush. It wasn't Kisha. He had spoken to her in the big house.

"This is Kuevee, my gardener," she said, when a man emerged into view.

Tedric stood up and shook the robot's hand. "Hello, Kuevee."

"You have seen my garden?"

"Yes, it's lovely, remarkable. Seen from the sky, coming down, it's even more amazing. One cultivated pocket in the middle of so much wildness. It's like one of Earth's ancient legends. I learned about it at the Academy. The Garden of Eden, where the first man and woman lived."

"It won't be the garden for long," Alyc put in. "I've written the Emperor, relinquishing all family rights. I want Milrod Eleven opened to colonization. I suppose, if I didn't do it myself, they'd do it to me before long."

"But you will keep the house and garden."

"If I'm allowed, yes."

"I'm sure that will be no problem." This was the first trace of resentment she had indicated concerning her family's changed status in the Empire.

"But what about Wilson?" she said. "You haven't told me about him."

Kuevee bowed and returned to his rounds. Tedric sat upon the narrow bench again. "That's a mystery to everyone. About a month ago, he simply disappeared from the palace. There was a report about a stolen ship, but I don't know if that was him or not."

"He was bored," she said. "I bet he just couldn't stand being decent. Born an outlaw, that's all he knows."

"I have heard about a ship of pirates supposedly operating in the Vylo Sector."

"Wilson, do you think?"

"I don't know. It's possible. The ship he took—if he took it—is a quick one."

"Then, if it is him, I say good luck. Do me one favor, Tedric. Don't catch him too soon. Let him enjoy himself. Let him be who he is. Wilson is a remarkable man—person. I think he should be free."

Tedric was shaking his head. "Whoever catches

him, it won't be me. As you know, I've a prior engagement."

"And how is my brother?" she said.

This was a more difficult question to answer. Matthew Carey, since his return to Earth after the battle in space, had cooperated with the victors in every possible way. He had made an immediate public statement, relinquishing any claim to the imperial throne, and had blamed his father for the circumstances leading to his original assumption of power. Because of this statement, Prince Randow had agreed not to punish Carey. He was living at court in the palace right now. But Tedric didn't trust him. There was something about Carey, something puzzling and mysterious, that continued to confuse him. He had never liked the man. What he felt now went considerably beyond dislike. Carey, in spite of the crushing defeat he had suffered, was too confident, cocky. He acted as if he knew things that others could only guess.

He answered Alyc as noncommittally as possible: "Matthew seems healthy enough. I see him perhaps once or twice a week. He speaks of you occasionally. He told me once that he intends to come to Milrod and see you as soon as Randow gives official leave."

"Did you believe that?"

The sharpness of her tone surprised him. "I don't know if I did or not."

"Well, I don't. You see, Tedric, I know Matthew and you don't. What he thinks of me is something I'd rather not describe. Put it this way. He's written me out of the family. If he never sees me again, it'll be too soon for him."

"That isn't what he said to me."

"It's not what he said to me, either. I met him once on Earth after we'd landed. He was polite and friendly. I never believed a word or a gesture."

"You're still his sister. That has to mean something."

"Not when it's only blood, and I'm sure, as far as Matthew's concerned, that's all it is or can be: just blood. A true Carey can't sit in one place as I have for all these years. He's got to be always battling, struggling, picking a fight with the universe. I'm too passive to be a Carey. I let things happen to me rather than forcing them to happen to others. I suppose my blindness is to blame. I sometimes think, if I could see, Father would have made me Empress Alyc. I always was his favorite."

"Then I'm almost glad that you are blind. If you were the enemy we'd faced on Earth, I doubt that we would have won the battle."

She smiled at his compliment. "For that, I thank you, but there is another thing. We've talked of many people and places, but I really did invite you here for a reason. Tedric, I've found out something very important. It's so incredible it almost frightens me to believe it."

"What?" But he knew. He had an idea. There

was only one thing she could mean. "It's your voices, isn't it?"

"I know what they are—who they are."

"Who?"

She spoke softly. "Ever since I returned here, it hasn't been the same. Not because Father is dead—he was seldom here when he was alive—but because I'm not the same. So I've been listening. To the voices. Not the way I used to, but really listening. I make notes. I think about what I've heard. And I remember what you told me on Earth when we were alone— about yourself—who you are, where you came from, why you think you're here. And, Tedric, I think I've found a solution. I know I have."

"What?"

"The voices—some of them—they're the Scientists."

"No," he said, but as soon as he uttered the word, he knew he was wrong and she was right. He might have guessed the truth before—perhaps only subconsciously. "Then that explains how you heard my name—my real name."

"It does."

"And it explains some other things—many other things. But . . . why? Is it their idea? Is it done on purpose?"

"I don't think so. I think the power is mine. They must know about it, if they're as powerful as everyone says, but I don't think they can control it. I read minds. They talk with their minds. That's why I hear them."

Tedric knew that part was true. He had met with the Scientists before, and they did not speak with their mouths; their lips never moved. "But why do you have this power and no one else?"

"Do you expect me to answer that? Because of my accident. Because of what happened to me when I saw the nova. I don't know, Tedric. I doubt that I ever will."

"Then it could be just an accident."

"I imagine that it is, yes."

"But, if you can hear them, what do they say? Have they spoken about me recently, about the red clouds?"

"They speak of you constantly. I'll show you the notes I've made. I'll tell you everything I can. But it's not easy. They don't use words. It's feelings mostly, like emotional pictures. The Scientists talk that way and so do the others."

"The others?"

"The Scientists are not the only voices I hear. There are two forces. If the Scientists are benevolent, then these others—these creatures—are evil. They hate you, Tedric, and want you dead."

In spite of the fierce gleam of the sun, Tedric felt a chill. The Scientists had hinted of the existence of a contrary force, but this was the closest he had come to glimpsing these powerful beings. "What can you tell me about them?"

"Not very much. Their voices are softer than those of the Scientists and I do not hear them often. And they speak indirectly. In riddles. I will tell you what I can, but I wish there were more. They have agents among us, the same as the Scientists do. They aren't human. I don't know what they are."

Tedric felt like a blind man suddenly permitted a brief, fleeting glimpse of the world of the sighted. But what could he do about it? He knew, no matter what, he would have to go on as he had.

Alyc suddenly said, "Tedric, I can help you."

He broke free of his own thoughts and said, "I know—you have."

She shook her head. "That's not what I mean. Tedric, when you leave Milrod, I want to go with you. I want to travel to the red cloud and beyond if necessary. I want to keep watch on them. On the Scientists —and on the others, too. Tedric, if you want to win, if you want to fulfill the destiny laid out for you by the Scientists, I think you need my help."

He understood what she was saying and why she was saying it, but of course there was no way he could agree. "You can't go with me."

"Isn't there room aboard the ship?" she said sharply.

He felt he owed her an honest reply. "Well, I suppose there is, but—"

"Is it my blindness? Are you afraid I'll bump into things?"

"No. Of course not. I know better than that."

"Then what is it? My age? My lack of experience? Because I couldn't get along without servants or robots?"

"No. I know that you're—"

"Is it Matthew? Are you afraid of him?"

"No, I'm not afraid of him," he said, with growing irritation.

"Then I know what it must be," she said bitterly. "There can be only one reason. It's propriety, isn't it? It's the established code of feminine conduct, the mores of the time, the odds against any woman doing anything except sitting at home and slowly dying. I'm sorry, Tedric, because I thought more of you. I thought, since you weren't born in this universe, you might be able to tell what is stupid and senseless and what is not. I thought it might matter that I have powers no man ever dreamed of possessing. That's why I invited you here. Now I'm sorry I did. I'm sorry I ever told you anything. I should have known. Telepathy isn't enough to alter the fact of my gender. If I were a man, you wouldn't hesitate one second. But I'm not that lucky. I'm just a woman, so I have to stay in this garden and wilt like a bush that everyone's forgotten to keep watered."

He felt like a fool. There were no words with which to defend his position, no way to deflect her bitterness. There was only one thing he could say that made any sense, and so he said it: "All right, Alyc. Then go with me."

Her face suddenly changed. Her whole aspect.

She was transformed. With a glowing smile, she said, "Do you really mean that?"

"After those names you called me, do you have to ask? Of course I mean it." He extended a hand and gripped hers. "Whenever you're ready to go, call me. After all that, there's no possible way I can leave this planet alone and manage to hold my head up without shame."

"Then I did it!" she cried.

"Did what?" He sensed that she was talking about something else.

"I beat the odds. Two hundred fifty billion-to-one, and I'm the one." Leaning over, she kissed him suddenly. "Thank you for everything."

END